Paint the Hills Red

Also by Ron Schwab

The Lockes
Last Will

Medicine Wheel

Hell's Fire

The Law Wranglers
Deal with the Devil

Mouth of Hell

The Last Hunt

Summer's Child

Adam's First Wife

Escape from El Gato

Peyote Spirits

The Coyote Saga
Night of the Coyote

Return of the Coyote

Twilight of the Coyote

The Blood Hounds
The Blood Hounds

No Man's Land

Looking for Trouble

Snapp vs. Snapp

Lucky Five
Old Dogs

Day of the Dog

Sioux Sunrise

Paint the Hills Red

Grit

Cut Nose

The Long Walk

Coldsmith

The Accidental Sheriff

Paint the Hills Red

Ron Schwab

Uplands Press

OMAHA, NEBRASKA

Uplands Press
1401 S 64th Avenue
Omaha, NE 68106
www.uplandspress.com

Publisher's Note: This is a work of fiction. Names, characters, places, and incidents are a product of the author's imagination. Locales and public names are sometimes used for atmospheric purposes. Any resemblance to actual people, living or dead, or to businesses, companies, events, institutions, or locales is completely coincidental.

Ordering Information:
Quantity sales. Special discounts are available on quantity purchases by corporations, associations, and others. For details, contact the "Special Sales Department" at the address above.

Uplands Press / Ron Schwab -- 2nd ed.

ISBN 978-1-943421-62-6

Chapter 1

DAN MCCLURE STARED at the blank canvas that was perched on the wooden easel in front of him, soaking in the warmth of the afternoon sun that caressed his naked back. He had moved his materials outside hoping that the fresh spring air would lift his black mood and release his creative juices. But although his mood had brightened, he had not yet touched a brush to the forbidding canvas. He knew what he was going to paint, but the first stroke of a new painting had always been agonizing. It was as though the virgin canvas resisted his touch, challenged him to invade its cloak of white. But inevitably he would confront the cold and unresponsive canvas and seduce it with all the love and tenderness he could muster, make it warm and pliable to his touch. He knew that, for in the end, the decision was simple: he had to paint.

He sat on a three-legged stool in the middle of the quiet, barren ranch yard with the oils on his palette turning dry and crusty in the sun. A gold-breasted meadowlark warbled from the corral fence near the barn and drew Dan's eyes away from the canvas. The bird beckoned him to take a walk through the ponderosa-studded hills that loomed behind the ranch buildings, and he surrendered easily. He stood up and placed his brush and palette on the stool. Then, like a drowsy mountain lion, stretched his tall, lean frame, working the stiffness out of his muscular arms and back. His arms stretched skyward like a savage praying to his gods.

Suddenly a rifle cracked from the trees behind him and drove a bullet into his back. The bullet hit him like a sledge, and he pitched forward, crashing into the easel and toppling over it before he sunk to the ground and collapsed atop the stretched canvas.

He lay there motionless, helpless, as a terrifying numbness spread over his back and consumed his body. He was dying, he thought, strangely unafraid as he drifted into darkness, and a river of blood snaked its way over his back and down his ribcage before dripping onto the white canvas and painting an expanding crimson lake there.

Chapter 2

THE TWO RIDERS reined in their horses at the sound of the gunshot and paused, listening as it echoed through the hills that surrounded the grassy valley in the heart of Nebraska's Pine Ridge country. Megan Grant might have been mistaken for an Indian as she sat astride her pinto gelding, clad in faded blue denims and a dusty, well-worn buckskin shirt, her straight raven hair falling from beneath a wide-brimmed Plainsman's hat and dropping to mid-back. From a distance, few would have guessed she was a woman, for in the saddle, her slight and slender figure gave her a boyish appearance.

She turned to her companion, a stocky, grizzled cowhand with a leathery face and deep bird-track creases extending from the corners of his eyes.

"That came from over by Ike Hanson's place," Megan said. "Winchester, I'd say."

Solomon Pyle shifted in his saddle and spat a brown, gooey wad of tobacco that made one cheek look like a chipmunk's. "Hunter, maybe. Them hills is fat with white-tail lately," he croaked in a gravel voice.

"Ike's place is deserted," she said. "He was fretting about squatters taking over when he moved to Omaha. Suppose we ought to take a look?"

The old man cocked his head to one side and, squinting against the sun, looked back at her poker-faced. "What if I say no?"

"I think I'll take a look anyway," she said tossing her head haughtily. Then she kneed her horse and took off at a dead run across the meadow. "Go on home, old timer," she called back. "You look tired." She gave her pinto free rein, and it flew through the lush grass at a fast, even gait, and she felt like a bird leaning into the gentle spring breeze with her hair flying about her neck and her body gliding easily with the motion of the horse. She did not look back again, for she knew that Sol would follow.

Solomon Pyle had been with her on the small ranch north of El Paso at her birth some twenty-one years before, and he had been there when her mother died five years later and again when Ben Grant pulled up stakes in

Texas and headed north for the new cattle country in the Nebraska Panhandle he had heard tales about. And he was still with her again little more than a year ago when she had arrived home and found her father, or what a sawed-off shotgun had left of him, sprawled in the open doorway of their ranch house.

Yes, Solomon Pyle had always been there. But why? She had a feeling there was a story that had not yet been told.

"Maggie, hold up," came Sol's voice as she neared the Hanson place.

There was an urgency in his voice that cautioned her, and she slowed the gelding while Sol caught up. When he drew even with Megan he gestured to the northeast toward a feathery plume of dust that hovered where a rider had just disappeared over the crest of a sandstone ridge. They slowed their horses to a walk.

"That fellar was goin' like a cat with his tail afire," Sol growled.

"But what would he have been shooting at?" she asked. "And why was he in such a hurry?"

"A man don't ride like that if he just took hisself a shot at a deer. He was high-tailing it away from Ike's place. While you was riding hell-bent for election, I saw him movin' on. If you'd spend more time looking and less time ridin' the hell out of that poor horse, you'd learn something, sis."

She pretended she did not hear his words. Sol was preaching again and a retort would simply trigger another sermon.

They came onto a wagon trail that left two shallow dimples in the grass and angled northward up the valley toward Ike Hanson's. When Megan saw the outline of the leaning, lopsided Hanson barn, she dug her boot heels gently into the gelding's flanks, and the horse lurched forward, ready to race again.

But Solomon Pyle called her up short. "Maggie, hold up, damn it!"

She obeyed, realizing instantly she was behaving like a giddy tenderfoot. What had gotten into her? She had better sense.

Sol sidled up next to her. "You let me ride in first. You trail me a ways behind. Be ready to back me up, just in case."

Her hand moved to the stock of her rifle, and she slipped it out of the saddle holster. Sol had taken charge now. It would be unthinkable to go against his instincts when danger might be near. She would subdue her rebellious streak for now. She had learned the hard way. For a fleeting moment she wondered again if Ben Grant might still be alive if she had not behaved so childishly and so impetuously the year before.

She shook off the thought and nudged the pinto up the wagon trail lagging some hundred feet behind Sol as he rode cautiously to the fringe of the ranch yard.

She could not make out Sol's face as his horse feinted to the right and then to the left. But she knew that those translucent, all-seeing eyes would be searching the surrounding terrain like those of a wary pronghorn approaching an open meadow. And Sol's nose would be twitching like a birddog's, too. He claimed he could smell trouble, sniff it out, within a mile. She more than half believed him.

He wheeled his horse toward her, waved her in, and turned back and galloped into the ranch yard. By the time she got there, the old cowboy had dismounted and was kneeling over the prostrate form of a man. A dead man, she thought. The scene reminded her of a steer slaughtering.

She dismounted and ran to Sol's side. The man lay ominously still. His ashen face was half-buried in the dry dust. The fresh thick blood that slicked his bare back flowed slowly in tiny rivulets that went across his flesh in all directions like a bloody spider web, finally forming crimson pools on the earth and the artist's canvas beneath him. "Is . . . is he dead?" she asked.

Sol dug an old kerchief out of his hip pocket and commenced clearing away the partially coagulated blood that the warm sun had already started baking on Dan McClure's back. "Nope. He's bad enough, but looks a hell of a lot worse than it is." Sol's fingers probed gently at the scarlet flesh a few inches to the left of Dan's spine and near the base of the ribcage where the bullet had entered. "Hardly bleeding here anymore." He leaned over and slid his hand along Dan McClure's ribcage and under his chest and then pulled it back. The hand was slippery wet with dark red blood. "I'll be damned," he said.

"What is it?"

"He's bleedin' like a stuck pig from his belly side. We gotta plug that quick or he's a gonner." Sol started to peel off his shirt, exposing faded red long johns. He slipped the Bowie knife out of its sheath at his waist and handed the knife and shirt to Megan. "Here, cut this up, sis. It ain't clean, but it's all we got."

As Megan fashioned crude compresses, Sol folded the bloodied kerchief and pressed it against the back wound and then rolled Dan gently over. "Whiter than a damn ghost," he mumbled.

"But his breathing's steady," Megan observed. She handed Sol a broad strip of soiled flannel.

Sol rolled the cloth up quickly and, with a deftness that belied his gnarled hands, pressed it against the bleeding, pulsating hole in Dan's belly. "He ain't dead yet, but come within a cat's whisker. Looks strong as a golderned bull."

He was a big man, Megan thought. Tall, very tall. And handsome in a rugged sort of way. Thick wiry hair, reddish-brown, almost the color of ponderosa bark. His face appeared chiseled and hard like Wyoming granite, and his arms and shoulders were thickly muscled although his body had a hungry-dog leanness to it. She wondered how old he was. Early thirties?

"Meggie, did you hear me? What in tarnation's gotten into you?"

She looked up. "What? Did you say something?"

"Good Lord, gal, are you deaf? I said there's a bucket over there by the well. Get some water and we'll try to clean this hombre up and see what he looks like under this mess. I need help, and there you are squattin' on your haunches eyeing him like he was a prized stallion."

She could feel the heat spread across her cheeks as they flushed with embarrassment, and then she bolted up. "All right, I'll get your damned water. There's no reason to get mean and crotchety about it."

"Ah, Meggie," Sol whispered to himself as she stomped off to retrieve the water. "What's to become of you? You're prime and in season, and we're hog-tied in these hills and in the middle of a range war to boot. This ain't no place for a young filly. Or a dried up old stud horse, either," he added, shaking his head resignedly.

"Just about got that blood dammed up," Sol said as Megan dabbed the moist cloth at the bloody torso. "Know what I think?" He didn't wait for an answer. "We just heard one shot. This hole ain't deep, just spitting a lot of blood. I think the damn bullet went in his back and rode his rib bone around the front and came out here. It knocked him loco, but if he didn't lose too much blood, he just might pull through."

"He'll pull through all right," Megan said firmly. "I know he will."

No sooner had she said it than Dan moaned and moved his head groggily from side to side. Megan dipped a fresh cloth in the bucket and placed it on Dan's fore-head. His eyes blinked several times and then opened. They seemed glazed with pain and confusion. And they were deep mahogany brown. She had hoped they would be brown.

Dan started to lift himself up, but fell back. Sol put a steadying hand on his shoulder. "Take it easy, son. We're friends. You'll be all right if you don't push yourself. But you ain't going no place for a few days."

Megan watched as the stranger tried to focus his eyes on Sol. "Who . . . what happened?"

"You took a slug in the back, son, but near as I can tell, the bullet went out on its own and didn't hit no vitals. You bled a bucket, though. You've got a couple of nasty wounds. I'll tell you straight out, you're gonna be a sick man for a spell. You'll feel a hell of a lot worse before you feel better, but I got a hunch you'll make it."

Dan shifted his body slightly and winced. "I don't know how I could feel much worse," he said.

"You will. Take my word for it."

"Sol," Megan scolded, "don't be such a pessimist. The man doesn't need that kind of talk right now."

"The man's entitled to the truth, Meggie. That's all I gave him."

Suddenly Megan was aware that the stranger was staring at her as if he had just, at that moment, become aware of her presence.

"The young lady's Megan Grant," Sol said. "She owns the Bar G that joins this place on the west. I'm Solomon Pyle. I work for Miss Grant. Sort of anyhow."

Without drawing his eyes away from Megan, Dan replied with a low, raspy voice, "I'm Dan McClure. I just bought this ranch. I moved in about a week ago." He turned his head back to Sol. "My first caller wasn't very friendly."

Sol rubbed the stubble on his chin with his free hand. "You didn't know about the trouble we got here?"

Dan's brow furrowed. "What trouble?"

"Well, that's another story, friend. It'll hold."

Megan was incredulous. This stranger bought Ike Hanson's place? Impossible. Ike would not have sold it without giving her first chance. They had been friends and neighbors. Ike's place had only two sections. Ike knew he could have set his price and the Bar G would have raised it some way. They would have mortgaged to the hilt if they had to. No, Ike would never have let the place go to a stranger.

Suddenly, she did not like this man. He was lying. She could restrain herself no longer. "You didn't buy this place from Ike," she snapped.

The man looked at her with those mahogany eyes. Eyes that now seemed to be trying to see what was behind her own. Eyes that made her unexplainably uneasy and skittish.

"Isaac Hanson, ma'am, that's the name of the old codger who sold it to me. We made the deal in Omaha. Check with the Land Office and see for yourself. I had the deed recorded before I ever saw the ranch."

"I will see for myself," she said. "I don't believe you. Ike wouldn't have done that. And buying it without seeing it . . . that's some tale, mister."

"It's the truth." Dan's voice faded and he slipped back into unconsciousness.

"Damn your hide, Meggie," Sol scolded. "Now look what you've done. You got no cause to pick a fight with this fellar. Least ways let him get back on his feet. I swear, sometimes you're meaner than a rattler on a hot skillet."

Megan cooled quickly. Sol didn't have to tell her that her temper had gotten the best of her again. "What are we going to do about him?"

"Well, I suppose if it was up to you we'd leave him here for the buzzards."

The old devil. He always had to have the last jab. "I'm sorry," she said. "I shouldn't have talked to him that way. But I do think he's lying."

"Liar or not, we can't leave him here."

"Should we take him over to our place?"

"We shouldn't move him no more than we got to. I see he's got a buckboard there, but if we juggle him in that for four or five miles, he'll be bleeding like a mountain creek again. No, we'd better put him up in his house. I can stay the night, but I want you to hightail it home be-fore nightfall. Tell the boys what happened and maybe post a guard tonight. Sounds like Dunkirk's gettin' set to stir things up again."

"How do we get Mr. McClure here in the house?" she asked. "We can't carry a man that size."

"Well, sis, if you can keep from cuttin' the poor devil up with your tongue, we'll just get him woke back up, and he'll have to help us out a little. You're right about that. There's too much man there for us."

Megan placed a cold compress on Dan's head again and as they worked to bring him back to consciousness, Megan said, "Did you notice these things on the ground?"

"I ain't blind, gal. Yep, I saw them. Never saw anything like 'em though."

"Do you know what they are?"

"I ain't much for games."

"They're an artist's things. An easel, a canvas. Over there in the dirt, they call that a palette. He mixes his paint on it. And this stool. He was painting."

"Painting? You mean like a picture?"

"Yes."

"I don't see no picture."

"He must have just been getting ready to work. He must be an artist."

"Hell, gal, you're crazy. A man like that? Look at him. Does he look like a fellar that'd spend his time drawing pictures?" Sol spat out the words contemptuously.

Megan had to agree. She had seen a painter once in Ogallala and had watched him work with fascination, but he had been a pale, spindly little man with tiny, almost feminine hands. This man's hands were large and powerful looking, but the evidence suggested that he did, indeed, paint. It somehow disappointed her and made her like him even less.

Chapter 3

MEGAN HEADED THE pinto at a gallop for the west end of the valley. She would just make it back to the Bar G before sundown. She had wanted to stay at Ike Hanson's. It would always be Ike Hanson's place to her, never Dan McClure's.

When McClure had awakened again, she wanted to interrogate him further, but he had not been up to talking much. It had been a struggle for them to get him into the house, for even conscious, in his weakened state he had not been much help. But half-pushing, half-shoving, they had gotten him through the door where they helped him to the straw mattress on the cot. Sol got a fire going in the fireplace, and she had found some dried beef and prepared a pot of skimpy broth before she left. McClure had passed out on the cot, and unless he woke up soon, the beef broth wasn't going to do him much good.

Sol said to let him sleep, that sleep was the best medicine now. And Sol was, no doubt, right, she admitted grudgingly. But the man could use something to eat, too. No wonder he looked half-starved; there was hardly a thing to eat in the place. If they were going to have to nursemaid Mr. McClure, she had better haul over some supplies in the morning. She didn't care about Dan McClure, she told herself, but she didn't want Sol starving to death while he was holed up there.

One thing she had established while in the house: McClure was indeed an artist. The house was scantily furnished, and it was obvious that the man did not indulge himself in luxuries. But the three rooms were crammed with paintings. Paintings resting on easels; paintings hanging on walls; paintings leaning against the walls. She had been awestruck and flabbergasted at what she had taken in with only a cursory survey of the rooms, but what she had seen fascinated and captivated her, and she wanted to see them again. She tried to recall now the paintings she had observed there, but everything was a blur in her memory except for two that were imprinted so indelibly in her mind that she could not forget them even if she tried. Both were portraits: one of a young, golden-haired woman holding an equally golden-haired little girl. Two of the most strikingly beautiful persons she had ever seen. Of course, she was seeing what the artist saw.

The other at first disgusted her and then strangely excited her. It was a portrait of a very naked, very voluptuous young woman poised suggestively on a satin-covered bed.

Chapter 4

DAN MCCLURE'S EYES opened and then shut again as they were blinded momentarily by the glare of the mid-morning sun that sifted through the dust-coated windows of the house. He tried to shift positions on the bed, but surrendered, weak and exhausted, to the knife-like pain that ripped through his back and chest.

"Just hold up a minute, young fellar," came a deep, raspy voice. "I'll give you a hand there."

Dan looked up at the weather-beaten face that hovered over him. The old man looked familiar. Where had he seen him before? What was he doing here? Then gradually it came back. He had been shot by some unknown assailant. This man and someone else, a young woman, had found him. He looked around the room trying to clear his head while the old man gently and expertly worked a folded blanket under his neck and shoulders, elevating his head and inching him out of the path of the sun's rays.

"How's that, son?" Solomon Pyle asked.

"Much better. Thanks, Mr. . . . . I'm sorry, I don't remember your name."

"Pyle. My handle's Solomon Pyle. I generally answer quickest to Sol."

"I guess I'm in your debt, Sol. I must have been in pretty bad shape when you found me."

"Yep, that you was. When I first saw you laying there, I thought you was dead as a can of corned beef. Guess you don't kill so easy, though." He straightened up and hobbled over to the fireplace. "We got to get something down your gullet and get your strength back. You ain't through this yet, but I figured you'd be a hell of a lot worse than this by now. Them wounds ain't festerin' up near as much as I looked for."

Dan let Sol Pyle do the talking while the venerable cowboy spooned the hot beef broth into his mouth. The warm liquid brightened him measurably and he felt a surge of strength, although his arms and legs still felt like they were weighted with lead.

"We'll get you on your feet for a little after a bit," Sol said. "You'll be stoved up for a month yet, and you're goin' to have to walk real careful like or you'll jostle things loose again. But you'll get better quicker on your feet than on your ass."

"Can you get a doctor out to look at me?"

"Hell, a sawbones couldn't do you no good. Besides, the nearest doc's up at Fort Robinson, and that's two days' ride by buckboard. You ain't torn up all that bad. We'll keep you doctored up, and you'll heal just fine. I'll stay with you nights for a spell yet. Meggie can look after you days."

"Meggie? Oh, the young woman who was with you."

"More wildcat than woman. She'll see that you don't get too rambunctious."

Dan swallowed the last spoonful of broth. "What I want to know," he said, "is who shot me and why?"

"You mean you don't know who it was?"

"No, I didn't see anybody, and I wouldn't have known who it was if I had seen him. Don't forget, I'm a newcomer here."

"You don't have any enemies on your trail?" Sol asked.

"No, I can't imagine who it could be."

"Damn, I feared you'd say that."

"I take that to mean you've got some ideas," Dan said.

"Wouldn't want to say," Sol drawled.

"Look, Mr. Pyle—"

"Sol. Nobody calls me mister, leastways not friends."

"All right, Sol. And I'm Dan. But put yourself in my shoes. If somebody put a bullet in your back and somebody else had an idea who it was, wouldn't you be pushing damned hard for some answers?"

The old man set the spoon and bowl aside. "Just don't want you goin' off half-cocked. Brought you back this far; hate to lose you now."

"You don't need to worry about that. I'm not an impulsive man."

Sol fished a stick of twisted chewing tobacco out of his hip pocket and took a chaw, ruminating like a cow with her cud for some moments before he spoke. "You for sure bought this land off Ike Hanson?"

"Yes. That's the name he gave me. He signed it 'Isaac' on the deed." Dan caught a glimpse of suspicion in Solomon Pyle's moss green eyes. "He was an old-timer. White hair, kind of a scrawny man, not more than five and a half feet tall. He had a gimpy leg. A rather cantankerous sort."

"Sounds like Ike all right. He pulled up stakes and went to Omaha to live with his daughter," Sol said.

"I know. That's where I met him. I was an agent with a land development company there. Hanson walked in a few months back and said he wanted to sell his ranch. Our company bought land all over Nebraska and resold it to investors, businessmen and ranchers. Something like a land clearing house, you might say. Anyway, when Hanson said his place was in the Pine Ridge country, my ears perked up. I knew the area. I was a cavalry officer with the Sioux expedition in the winter of '74, and I was stationed at Camp Red Cloud Agency before they changed the name to Camp Robinson. I knew Lieutenant Robinson, by the way, the one they named the fort for. We shared a bottle of whiskey together just a few days before he was killed at Little Cottonwood Creek. I always vowed I'd come back to this country someday. Somehow it got in my blood and couldn't get it out of my system. I always knew sooner or later I'd end up here. I wanted to paint the Pine Ridge and Black Hills and the Rockies. Not just the scenery, but the people and their way of life. I have a feeling that we're living in a time and era that won't last long. A hundred years from now, people are going to look back and say those were a special breed of people that lived in the West then. That's what I want to capture on canvas. Do you understand what I'm saying?"

"Nope, but you sure as hell can talk a scab off a blister when you get started. Near as I can tell you still ain't told me how you came to buy this ranch."

If Solomon Pyle was one thing, he was blunt. It had been so long since Dan had had human company he guessed he had started running off at the mouth without realizing it.

"When I talked to Mr. Hanson," Dan said, "I asked him if he had any neighbors who might be interested in purchasing the ranch. He said he did, but that he didn't want to sell it to any of them. He was afraid he'd just get everybody upset if he picked one over the other. He said he didn't want to be responsible for getting anyone killed. I thought he was joking; I didn't take him seriously. Looks like maybe I should have. Anyway, I took it as kind of an omen that it was time for me to move on. I asked Hanson if he'd sell me the ranch. I'd made some money in land development and had enough to buy the ranch and maybe live for a year or so. That was one time in my life I acted on impulse, I guess. Anyway, I stayed with the company long enough to finish off my work and then I packed up my paintings and headed for my ranch. My ranch that I'd never seen until I got here."

"Ike didn't sell you much of a place, did he? No offense meant, but he couldn't afford no hands, and he was too old and feeble to look after things proper."

"All I wanted was the land to live on, and I wasn't disappointed. I don't think there's a better spot in the whole Pine Ridge. The whole country for that matter. The buildings I can do something about with time and hopefully, someday, a little money. This country's just the way I re-membered it when I left eight years ago. I'll never leave it. I'll never leave this ranch. I know what I want now, and I spent too much of my life trying to find out. This time I'm staying put."

Sol shook his head doubtfully. "I hope you're right, friend. Anyhow, seeing as how you think you're here to stay, I'd better tell you just what kind of trouble you bought along with this here ranch. A heap of it, believe me. I can't figure Ike not telling you. Of course, he could be a crafty old bird when it came to a dollar. We had talked to Ike about leasing the place, and he said he'd let us know on it. No way he would have sold out to Woody Dunkirk, and the other ranchers hereabouts are already mortgaged to their butts. Meggie wants this place in the worst way, but hell, the Bar G couldn't come up with a respectable down payment these days, and Ike would have knowed that. Nope, Dunkirk's got enough money to burn a wet mule. Wasn't nobody else to bankroll this ranch. I suppose that's why Ike went and sold the place to a stranger."

"Dunkirk," Dan said. "You don't sound like you have much affection for the man. Who is he? Does he have some connection with my taking a bullet?"

"In this man's opinion, Dunkirk's crooked as a rattle-snake and twice as dangerous. A rattler gives you warning: Dunkirk don't."

"Are you suggesting he's the one who ambushed me?"

"Not as such. Dunkirk don't dirty his own hands with that sort of thing. He's got gun hands to do his bush-whacking. But I'd bet a year's wages that the fellar who shot you is on the Diamond D payroll."

"But why would this Dunkirk want to have me killed? I don't even know the man."

"Because you own this ranch."

"I don't understand."

"Well, Mr. McClure . . . Dan . . . Ike Hanson sold you a passel of trouble. Hell, Dunkirk would have done him in a long time back if the old fool hadn't been so sickly and worn out that Dunkirk figured he'd waste away on his own soon enough. Old Ike, though, he wouldn't die. Tough as a patch of buffalo grass."

"But this is just two sections . . . 1,280 acres. Nothing compared to what a man like Dunkirk must own."

"True enough. At last count, Dunkirk had 40,000 acres of grass and was still adding on. Of course, he's not greedy. Just wants the land that's next to his, that's all."

"And the Bar G doesn't?" Dan asked cynically.

"You got yourself a point, Dan. I suppose most ranchers have got a little bit of land hog in 'em, but most won't kill for a few acres of grass. Dunkirk will."

Dan shifted on the cot, working his hip into a depression in the mattress. "You've never said why Dunkirk wants this place."

"Ride out and take a look at your ranch, Dan. You're the hooking cow, and as far as Dunkirk's concerned, you've got to be dehorned."

"You're talking in riddles, Sol. What's a hooking cow?"

"It's a cow with long, sharp horns, generally a sneaky old bitch. She'll stand out on the range chomping on the grass, biding her time real peaceful like when the cowboy rides by, payin' her no account 'cause she's such a nice old cow. Then, first thing you know, she comes up from behind and takes his horse, maybe gores herself a cowhand as an afterthought. I'm thinking Dunkirk sees this place as the hooking cow."

"Why?"

"Water. If there's one thing in these parts worth more than good grass, it's good water. You've got Dunkirk land touching you on all sides excepting one, on the west where Meggie's place joins. Dunkirk's trying to crowd out dozens of small ranchers. There was twice as many a few years back. But Ike Hanson's place and the Bar G, they always really stuck in Dunkirk's craw because, between them, they could shut off the only dependable water supply for better than 10,000 acres of Dunkirk's best grazing land. No water, no cattle."

"You mean he's afraid we might dam up the creeks and cut off his water supply?"

"Yep, you especially. Take yourself a look at the county plat map and you'll see that you and the five thousand acres held by the Bar G look sort of like a key hole with square corners, pretty much surrounded on all sides by the Diamond D. Well, you happen to be sitting on a pocket of underground springs that break through the ground and feed the creeks with all the water they can handle, winter and summer, rain or drought. Your little spread's right at the end of that key hole. The creeks join up and go on to Dunkirk's land through a little bottle-neck canyon that breaks through the hills from your land. Wouldn't take five men more than a couple of days to shut that water off and make yourself a big lake so's you could let Dunkirk have water only when you wanted to. Sell it to him, maybe. He's got water of his own to get him through wet years, but you get a dry year or two, and you could have ol' Dunkirk by the balls."

"But I wouldn't do that. I wouldn't shut off his water supply. I was trained as an engineer at West Point. I know there's not much law on these things out here yet, but I think there are limits on how much you can impede the natural flow of water."

"There ain't much law of any kind around here. What we do have is owned by Dunkirk. Besides, Dunkirk don't know you wouldn't try to cut off the water. It ain't everybody that looks at things the way he does. If he was in your boots, he'd shut off that creek faster than chained lightning with a link snapped. Then he'd squeeze the rancher who needed the water till he could buy him out."

Dan was dubious. Solomon Pyle sounded like a man with a personal grudge that went beyond a dispute over water rights. "I don't know, Sol. It's still pretty hard to swallow that a man would kill over something like that. It's 1882. Nebraska's had statehood for close to twenty years. We're getting civilized out here."

"That's probably what Custer said when he was killed just a ways north and west of here not five years back," the old man growled. "Ask Megan about it. Ask her who blew her daddy's guts all over their front porch with a shotgun a year back. Ask a half dozen other small ranchers who've lost somebody to a bushwhacker in the past two years."

"If you're so sure it's Dunkirk, why don't you go to the law? There's a sheriff at the county seat in Medicine Hill. I saw his office. It was next to the land office."

"We can't prove nothin' and even if we could, it wouldn't do no good. I told you, Dunkirk owns the law."

"I don't believe that. Nobody owns the law. One man, maybe, but if the sheriff won't do his job you can go to the Attorney General or the Governor for help."

"Like hell. Not with the spindly vote we got out here in the Panhandle."

"I'll tell you this much," Dan said, "when I'm up and around, I'm going to make a call on the sheriff."

"It's a waste of time."

"We'll see. And I'll have a talk with Dunkirk, too. I just want to be left alone so I can get back to work."

"You're just askin' to get your fool head blowed off. If you go see Dunkirk, you just as well offer to sell the place. He'll give you four or five times what you paid. You can move on with some jingle in your pocket. Find you a place where you ain't so likely to pick up another case of lead poisoning."

"I already told you I'm staying here. I've made my last move."

"From the way you're going on, you won't be movin', that's for sure. You'll be eatin' worms out by one of them ponderosa before the summer's out."

Chapter 5

WITH WHAT DAN had learned was her typical bluntness, Megan Grant had announced the previous day, "After tomorrow, you're on your own. Sol and I don't have time to nursemaid orphan calves. We've got branding and castrating to get done."

"I understand," Dan had replied. "I'm grateful for all you have done."

"Do you want to rent out your grazing land this season?" she had asked, shifting the subject abruptly.

"I haven't given it any thought."

"We wouldn't overstock it, and we'd pay going cash rent. We couldn't pay you till fall, though, after we sell off some of the steer calves and cull the old cows. But if you don't rent it out, you won't have any income from it anyway. It would be a good deal for both of us. I didn't bring it up because you owe us anything. You could probably strike a better bargain with the Diamond D."

"Why would I want to deal with Dunkirk?"

"Money. And it might be a whole lot safer. Of course, maybe you want to sell out. I'd make a fair offer. I can't compete with Dunkirk if you want cash. You'd have to carry some of it."

"Look, Miss Grant, I'd appreciate it if you'd quit throwing this Dunkirk in my face. I'm not selling the land. I'm staying here. And I'll rent you the grazing land."

"I'll draw up the lease and bring it over tomorrow," she had said.

"I won't sign it. I said you can rent it. I'll take your word on the going rate, and you can pay next fall."

"But that's not good business," she had protested.

"You don't trust me?"

"I don't know yet. I just like to do things in a business-like way."

"Well, I'm sorry. I'm an artist, not a businessman. If you want your cattle to graze the land, you'll have to do it my way."

* * *

Dan swung his legs off the cot and stood up, straightening his body carefully, testing the soreness in his back and ribs, slowly working out the stiffness before stepping across the room to ferret out some clothes to cover his nakedness before Megan Grant arrived. On second thought, maybe he ought to greet the saucy young woman in his birthday suit. It would be interesting to catch the look on her face if she walked in on him like this. It might be something to capture on canvas.

Damn, she was a strange one, he thought. Hardly a congenial word had passed between them over the past ten days. The first week Sol had stayed over nights. Beneath the facade of the old man's gruff manner, Dan had discovered a warm human being who had sensitivity and shrewdness that Sol Pyle, for some reason, tried to hide. He would have to paint Sol someday soon.

But while he had fashioned a friendship of sorts with Sol and learned a great deal about the ranch foreman who had saved his life, Megan Grant was still an enigma to him. She was as aloof and standoffish as the first day they met. She had changed the dressings on his wounds twice daily, and she had fed him better than he had eaten for months: fresh baked bread, beef steak, strawberry pie. She had cleaned the house, such as she could, maneuvering around the easels and stacks of paintings scattered helter-skelter about the rooms. She had tended to the horses and for the past few days had spent a good deal of time outside, apparently, from the sound of the rapping hammer, looking to some of the repairs he had found so easy to put off.

But there was a barrier between them that imposed formality, made them guarded and wary. It was "Miss Grant" and "Mr. McClure." When she spoke, she tended to snap or bait, and he invariably responded in kind. Silence seemed to work best for them. Still, he thought, as he buckled his belt, he could never quite kick Megan Grant out of his head, and he spent too damn much time thinking about her. Maybe any woman would have done that to him now. Perhaps it was just the simmering, unsatisfied lust within him and not some nobler attraction for a woman that he found so unsettling. Whatever it was, he could not deny the existence of Megan Grant.

He tossed a few sticks of white ash on the dying embers in the stone fireplace. He would try to have a red-hot bed of coals by the time Megan Grant arrived. She was bringing a buckboard full of supplies today, she said, and she would fix breakfast. After that she was done with him.

He pulled the burlap curtain aside—the curtain Megan Grant had installed—and peered out the window. A gray cloud hung over the valley; it looked like they might get some rain before the day was out. And according to Sol, it was badly needed. It had been a dry winter and a dryer spring. And the grass would not thicken until a good gully washer swept over the Pine Ridge. Grass. Water and grass. They were the lifeblood of these hills.

He caught a glimpse of Megan's team and buckboard crawling down the wagon trail before he let go of the curtain and reached for his denim shirt. He slipped on the shirt as he stepped out on the porch and onto the ranch yard where he stood and waited. The wagon dragged some behind the horses, Dan observed. It evidently carried a heavy load. He ambled slowly out to meet her as the wagon rolled into the yard.

Megan disarmed him momentarily when she flashed an uncertain smile before she sprang off the wagon. Then, as she moved to the rear of the buckboard, her mood seemed to shift, and she shot him a reproachful glance.

"Good morning, Mr. McClure," she said coolly.

"Good morning. You've got quite a load there. Let me give you a hand."

"No, you go back in the house. You can't do any lifting yet."

"I feel fine," he protested, "and you can't unload all this yourself."

"Yes, I can," she said. "And don't be foolish. I can't waste any more time looking after things over here. If you don't use some common sense, you'll overdo it and end up flat on your back again."

"Miss Grant, you're treating me like a child."

"You're acting like one."

Damn, the woman's tongue could cut leather and there was no reasoning with her.

"All right, I'll go on in, but let me take some of the smaller items. I won't exert myself, I promise." He nodded toward the supplies. "What is all this anyway? I'm just one man."

"Coffee, flour, staples and canned goods that should see you a month. There's a slab of cured venison and some beef jerky. Somebody will try to drop some fresh meat off once in a while. The sacks are full of grain for the horses. You ran out a week ago in case you didn't know. They need grain. The grazing isn't good enough yet. I don't know what you planned to feed those animals, let alone yourself."

"I was intending to go into Medicine Hill for supplies."

"Sol said you were an army man. You should have known that you don't let yourself run that low in this country."

"I had other things on my mind."

She handed him a sack of coffee beans and a tin of sugar. "Like painting pictures?"

He caught the scorn in her voice. "You don't approve?"

"I don't approve or disapprove. It's not my business. But it seems to me a man ought to tend to making a living first and looking after his land if he's going to own it. This ranch you bought yourself . . . my father tried to buy it from Ike the day we moved in from Texas. Dunkirk and a lot of others would like to add this place to their holdings, and it grates me that you don't appreciate what you've got here."

She had her arms loaded now and they walked together to the house. "But I do appreciate it," he said. "I said I'd never leave. I figure I've got me a piece of heaven on earth right here."

"If you feel that way, you ought to take care of it then. These buildings need to be put back into shape. Ike didn't keep up his fences worth a damn, and that's going to make trouble with your neighbors if you don't do some fence work pretty quick. I suppose if the Bar G is going to rent your grazing land, we'll have to fix your fence, too."

"You guessed right, Miss Grant, because I don't intend to while away my summer fixing fences. You just do what has to be done and deduct the materials from the rent you owe me."

"What about the time?"

"That's your problem. I'm renting you the grass with the understanding that you'll keep up the fence."

"That wasn't part of the bargain."

"You don't have to rent it. Like you said yourself, there are plenty of others who would like to graze this land. As for the buildings, they'll just have to wait till I decide to make time. I've got to make up my mind what I'm going to do with this ranch over the long term anyway. I may want to run my own herd. That would make a difference on what I decide to do with the buildings."

"This place is too small to run your own herd. You can't run enough cows to make it pay, especially if you're going to spend your time painting pictures."

Dan bristled. "You know, Miss Grant, about my paintings . . . you said a little bit ago it wasn't any of your business. Well, I'm inclined to agree."

Chapter 6

MEGAN GRANT HAD outdone herself on the breakfast: ham, fresh eggs, biscuits, honey. Dan had added a pot of steaming hot black coffee. It was midmorning before Megan, with Dan's token assistance, had unloaded the buggy, and it was close to noon now as they both sat silently at the sturdy oak table, the one furnishing in the ranch house that Dan valued as a reminder of another life and time. They had barely spoken since their earlier sparring, and now they ate silently with the soft clicking of their utensils against their tin plates seemingly the only sound in the house. Dan cast a furtive glance at Megan across the table. She ate slowly, her eyes downcast as though absorbed in the mechanics of eating. He wondered if he could persuade her to sit for a portrait despite the apparent disdain she had for art. Or was it just artists she disliked?

There were not many women like her in this part of the country. There were transplants from other cultures—the East, or in many cases, Europe—and there was a place for them in his work. But Megan Grant was a child of the West, unscathed by any other influence in her upbringing. Could he capture her untamed spirit on canvas? What a challenge that would be.

He fixed his eyes on Megan now, studying her. She was beautiful in her own way. It was not the soft, gentle beauty that Larisa had carried with such grace. Not the kind of beauty one found in a satin gown in a grand ballroom. No, it was hard to imagine waltzing across a dance floor with Megan Grant.

Her smooth dark skin suggested Spanish ancestry, and it glowed with the sheen of a healthy, wild creature. Her supple frame exuded hardness, toughness, strength. She challenged a man, dared him to prove she was not his equal. She was a breed apart and Dan had never encountered a woman like her. What kind of man could she love? Certainly not a weak man.

He wished she would look up. He wanted to see her eyes again, those fascinating eyes that were a monochrome of green. In the dusky room, they were dark like lush, shaded grass. But in the afternoon sun, they would turn to the shimmering aqua of a turbulent ocean. Her eyes changed color with each mood and setting, probably with each season. How would he ever paint such eyes?

A low rumbling, like a mountain lion's morning growl, jarred him from his musing, and then a clap of thunder roared and shook the house. Megan looked up. "I'd better harness the team and try to beat this storm home," she said, but even as she stood up, the droplets of rain commenced pattering against the wood shingles and, in a matter of moments, the rain exploded from the sky in waves and sheets.

"There's the gully washer Sol's been praying for," Dan said. "You can't head out of here right now."

"But I need to get back to the ranch."

"You wouldn't get any work done with this rain anyway," he said. "Besides, it's dangerous traveling in weather like this. Wait till it lets up."

She suddenly seemed nervous and skittish, and she went to the window and looked out. Then she turned back to him, her face glum. "I guess I'd better wait a little while."

As he helped her clear the table and wash the plates, it occurred to Dan that Megan Grant, imprisoned with him in the house now, was edgy and unsure, like a caged animal, waiting for the chance to bolt out an open door.

It made him sorry that he had exchanged barbs with her earlier, and he resolved to ease her temporary captivity.

"I'm afraid I was a little gruff earlier," he volunteered. "You and Sol saved my life, and you've done more than any man has the right to expect of his neighbors. I apologize, and I hope I can pay you back some way."

"There's no debt," she said. "We'll present a bill for supplies but the rest, well, that's just something folks have to do for each other out here if we're going to survive."

"I see." He picked up the steel poker and knelt down to stir the embers in the fireplace. "I think I'll toss on a few more logs. The dampness is starting to make a chill in the house."

"Mr. McClure?" Megan asked.

He looked up. "Yes?" Her eyes had softened and looked sad somehow. Remorseful? He doubted it.

"Since I'm stuck here for a spell, I wonder if you would mind showing me your paintings."

He eyed her skeptically and tossed the logs on the fire before rising. "Sure. I'll be glad to show you. I just thought coming in and out of the house you would have seen them all."

"Well, I've glanced at them, but I've never taken a close look. I never got the chance to study them."

He led her through the cluttered rooms, skimming some of his work but pausing at some length at a painting from time to time to tell her about the history or setting, or to relate an anecdote about his inspiration. She was either genuinely interested, he thought, or an excellent actress, for her eyes leaped from intent appraisal to sparkling pleasure as they toured his cluttered gallery, and although she was obviously not schooled in art, her questions were intelligent and pointed, and she appeared to have some inborn sense of what was good and what was mediocre. She was candid in expressing her opinions, but her criticism and occasional praise, was almost always on the mark.

"How long have you been doing this?" she asked

"I can't remember when I didn't. I started sketching when I was a small child. We lived on a farm in the Ohio Valley. My first sketch was of a cow on a barn door. My father didn't approve of my wasting time on such things, but my mother was a piano teacher, a very sensitive woman, and she encouraged me. She always got her way with Dad anyhow, but I think he was always a little disturbed by my paintings. I guess he thought of my drawings as something of a perversion. I remember he would get embarrassed as hell when my mother would drag out some of my sketches and show them off to company."

"Did you attend an art school?"

"Eventually. I got an appointment to West Point when I was seventeen. I was trained as an engineer. Of course, after graduation it was the army's logic that I be assigned to cavalry."

"You told me you had served at Fort Robinson."

"Yes, in the early days. There were some bad times. I fought the Sioux. I can't say that I'm proud of it. But I fell in love with the West during that time. I want to trek into the Rockies and see—and paint—more of this country and its people, but this will be home."

"You said you had training."

"Yes, after I was discharged from the service, I studied art for a year at Yale. It helped, I think. I learned techniques that have given my work more sense of depth and reality. And I think I'm better with colors now. I know I approach my painting more systematically. But in the end, it's still something that comes from within you, and you can't teach that. Five artists will paint the same person five different ways. A good artist paints a close physical likeness, but a great artist will capture the soul or at least his conception of it. To me, that's the challenge whether I'm doing a portrait or a landscape or anything else."

"Have you sold many of your paintings?"

"Only a few. I've given more away to friends than I've sold. Until now, it's always been something I've done nights or between jobs. I've sent some of my work to a dealer in St. Louis. He thinks it will sell. I'm not so sure. I'll give it a year or two, but if I can't sell my paintings, I'll have to try to make a living some other way. But I'll stay here, and I'll keep painting when I can. I have to."

She paused by one of the portraits. "This one," she said, "I noticed it the first time I was here. Tell me about it. No, don't. . . . Let me guess." She stepped back from the painting, studying the golden-haired woman and the sleeping girl she cradled in her lap.

Dan had intended to hurry past this painting. He had been reluctant to discuss this one, but the excitement that glittered in Megan Grant's jade eyes pleased him, for the one joy that exceeded self-appreciation of his work was the sight of someone else receiving pleasure from it.

"You did it here," she said, smiling warmly at him, her face radiant.

"Did what?"

"It's not just a painting showing two people. You caught their souls. You're telling a story about them." She wrinkled her brow and suddenly looked serious. "That makes you great, doesn't it?" She crinkled her nose and smiled impishly.

He grinned sheepishly, "Yeah, I guess so. But you were going to tell me about them."

She turned back to the portrait, her eyes narrowing as she dissected it. "The child's tired out, but it's a happy tired. She's been playing, and she feels very safe in her mother's arms." A strangely wistful look came over Megan's face at the remark. "The woman is her mother, isn't she?"

"Yes, of course."

"I've never seen a lady so beautiful, and she's very refined. I could never be a woman like that, but, oh, how I envy her right now. She's very gentle and quite warm. She has what some folks call breeding. But she's not a snob. Her child, of course, is very dear to her, and they're so at peace. . . . I'd call it 'Portrait of Peace.' Oh, my—"

"What is it?"

"She loves the artist! She loves you, and you love her and the little girl. Why, of course, she's your child. And the woman must be your wife." She looked at him, her eyes wide with astonishment. "I didn't know you—"

"The woman's name was Larisa. And the little girl was Emily. I lost them four years ago. Diphtheria took Emily. The doctor thought Larisa died of the same thing. But I thought it was a broken heart. She didn't have the will or strength to fight back like some might."

"I'm sorry. I didn't mean to open old wounds."

"Don't be. I've come to terms with it. . . . As much as you ever can, anyway. They're a part of happy memories, but I try not to dwell on them, and I've learned not to live in the past."

They moved on, Dan caught unaware by the sensitivity and perceptiveness that had surfaced in Megan Grant. She was indeed a more complex woman than he had initially thought. She may have gleaned a great deal about his life from her study of Larisa's portrait, but he had learned much from her reaction to it.

"I'm curious about this one," Megan said, leading him to one of the few nudes. "I haven't decided if I like it, but it interests me."

Oh, God, she had picked Angela's portrait. He considered it one of his better works for mood and detail, but he knew its commercial market lay more in a Western saloon than in an Eastern gallery. He felt awkward standing in front of the provocative nude with this young woman who was not so many years beyond girlhood.

Unlike the portrait of Larisa and Emily, this one, he supposed, he would part with one day. But staring at it now, he called up fond memories of the delightful woman portrayed there. She looked back at him now, the lewd playful gleam in her ocean-blue eyes and knowing smile on her slightly parted lips. Raised up on one elbow, she rested her head with catlike laziness against her hand, patiently enticing her prey to move closer and within her grasp. Her rust red hair shone brightly against the green satin bedspread, and her milk-white skin enhanced the other colors, evoking a sense of bright color contrasts not often found in portraits. Her perfect sculptured breasts detailed to the tiny red scar above one nipple; the sweeping, provocative curves of her hips and thighs; the slender, tawny legs, one lifted discreetly to partially shield the matching foliage between her thighs. But any man would know what lay there. And even though, through familiarity, he should have been immune to Angela's charms, she cast a spell upon him even now.

They were silent for some moments, and Dan was reluctant to speak first. Megan appeared mesmerized by what she saw on the huge canvass, but this time he could not tell what she was thinking, whether she liked it or was repulsed by it. Certainly she was not bored.

"I used to see a picture of a naked lady in the saloon in Medicine Hill when I'd go to get Sol and my dad after I finished shopping. She wasn't anything like this. She was heavier and larger. Do you know what I mean?"

"Yes, I think so. Sometimes we call it Rubenesque."

"Yes, I've read of Rubens," Megan said. "But the painting in the saloon was so different. There was no detail, no individuality in the woman. She could have been anybody. Her eyes, for instance, they were just brown almonds: you didn't know if they were laughing or sad or angry."

"I understand."

"Well, that painting never really bothered me because I could never see the woman as anyone in particular. But this woman is different. She's a real person. Somebody you knew. And you didn't paint her from your imagination or a picture in a book, did you?"

"No."

"Is she a . . . harlot?"

"I suppose that's what some people would call her, but I always thought of Angela as a companion and friend. She was a very dear friend of mine during a very difficult time."

"I see . . . or I'm trying to."

"What do you think of her?"

"I don't know why, but I like her. But I don't know if I like the painting."

"Why not? Is it the nakedness that bothers you?"

"Yes . . . yes, I suppose that's it. I don't feel comfortable with it, and still I don't find it vulgar."

"I hope not. It wasn't intended to be."

"I guess what I think doesn't matter."

"I'm interested in what you think."

"Well, I really don't know what I think. When I decide, I'll tell you."

"Good. At least I can be confident you won't spare me."

She gave him a wry smile. "I guess I haven't so far, have I?"

She could laugh at herself. He liked that in a person. At least their relationship had prospects of turning civil. She turned away from the painting.

"Let's move on," she said. "I have a feeling Angela's laughing at me."

"She's probably laughing at herself," Dan said. "That was more like Angela."

As they finished meandering through the paintings, Megan said, "How can you paint here? It's so crowded. And the house is so dingy. Don't you need more light?"

"Yes, that's why you found me in the yard after I was shot. And that's why I have to ignore some of the other ranch chores for now. I want to build a studio onto the house, one with more window space for natural light. It's important that I get it done before the weather turns cold again. Then maybe I can make this part of the house more livable."

"We can probably spare some hands for a spell after roundup."

"That would help a lot for the heavy work. I plan to ride into Medicine Hill to find a carpenter to direct things. I have the plans sketched out, and I've already talked to the man at the saw mill about the lumber."

"It sounds like you are here to stay, Mr. McClure. I'm afraid I didn't take you seriously at first." She walked to the window and peeked out again. "The rain's let up. I'd better start for home."

"But it's still heavy," he protested. "Maybe you should wait. You could get mired down in the mud someplace or get caught in a flash flood."

"I'll steer clear of the creek, Mr. McClure, and I know this country. I'll stay away from the mud holes."

"Don't take me wrong, Miss Grant, but you could stay the night if you need to. We could improvise suitable accommodations."

"No. Sol will be worried sick if I don't show up by nightfall. He'd have to ride over and be sure I was all right. At his age, I don't like to see him out in this kind of weather."

"He's more than just a foreman to you, isn't he?"

"I can't remember when Sol wasn't a part of my life. It was always like I had two fathers."

"He's an interesting man. I'd like to paint him. Do you think I could convince him to sit for a portrait?"

She smiled and shook her head. "I don't know. He's not much good at sitting still for anything. If you really want to, you'd better let me persuade him. I usually get my own way."

"I want to, and I'd appreciate your help, Miss Grant."

"You've got it, but I want the first option to buy the painting. And Mr. McClure, if you prefer, you may call me Megan."

"If you'll call me Dan."

"It's a deal, Dan. And now, I really must go. Do you need your dressings changed before I leave?"

"No, I can take care of it when I need to. And besides I'm on my own now, remember?" He hesitated. "Megan, there is something else I would like to ask."

"What is it?"

"Would you consider sitting for a portrait?"

"Me? Why me?"

"I'm always looking for new Western subjects, and I see you as very Western."

"What kind of portrait?" she asked suspiciously.

He blushed slightly when he caught the innuendo in her voice. "A respectable portrait. Probably wearing what you're wearing right now."

"I do own a few dresses."

"That's not what I want for this portrait. Would you consider it?"

"Not now. I'm still not too sure about you or your painting business. I don't feel comfortable with the idea. Perhaps I'm afraid of what you might see in me. I'll work on Sol for you. Then we'll see about me."

"Then you're not saying no."

"I'm not saying yes, either." She reached for the saddlebags that were draped over the chair and pulled out an old army poncho. She slipped her head through the hole in the cloak, donned her hat and slung the saddle bags over her arm.

"Megan, I have a suggestion," Dan said. "Why don't you leave your buckboard and team here and take one of my horses. You'll get home faster and you won't have to worry about the mud."

"I was going to ask you about that," she said. "Yes, I'll do that."

"Take the bald-faced gelding. He's a strong horse."

"All right." She headed toward the door and then stopped, turning and facing him. "Thanks for showing me your paintings, Dan. I'm glad it rained."

"Me too, and I hope we can be friends."

She nodded agreement, whirled and went out the door.

He followed her out to the porch and stood there watching after her as she sloshed across the ranch yard toward the barn. He waited until she emerged from the barn astride the gray bald-face. She reined the horse toward the house, lifted her hand in farewell as she approached, tugged her hat over her forehead, and headed the horse at a gallop into the driving rain.

Chapter 7

MEGAN DID NOT see the shadowy form of the rider as he slipped out of the cedar grove and fell in behind her. Her sure-footed gelding picked its way up the narrow trail that snaked up the slope and led over the rocky ridge that formed a natural boundary line between much of the west side of Dan Mc-Clure's sections and the Bar G ranch. The trail was easy to negotiate under normal conditions, but tonight it was muddy and slippery and a misstep could send horse and rider plummeting down the hillside: an almost certain broken leg for the horse, probably worse for the rider if she did not fall clear.

Megan squinted her eyes against the rain that pummeled her face and shivered as the water-drenched garments that clung to her skin began to soak a chill into her bones. She should have stayed the night at Dan Mc-

Clure's, and the thought that they could be sharing the warmth of an ash fire right now made her curse her foolishness for venturing into the storm.

No sooner had she left Dan's house than the rain had erupted again in torrents, and between fighting the mud and the wind and the thunder-skittishness of the bald-face, she had progressed toward home at a snail's pace. It would be nearly sundown if she could see the sun, and the darkness made her ride gloomier as well as more treacherous. She struggled to concentrate on the long, nearly invisible trail ahead of her, but her thoughts kept turning to Dan McClure. Until this afternoon, she had been dubious about his work and had looked somewhat contemptuously upon a man who would waste his energy on such an impractical pursuit. There was so little tangible to what he did, and the men she had been surrounded by all her life were physical men. She had judged a man's worth on how fast he drew a gun and his accuracy with his rifle, how well he could rope a calf, how many hours he could sit in a saddle. Their goals were sensible ones: roping more cattle, upgrading the quality of the horse herd, and buying more acres. Dan McClure did not fit that mold, and she had been wary of him because of it.

She was not certain what to think of him now, but she saw him in a different light, for the paintings and the peculiar reverence with which he had talked about them left her confounded. As she had studied his paintings with more than a causal eye, she felt as she moved from one to another that she was stripping him naked piece by piece, seeing more of Dan McClure than she wanted to see of any man, learning more about the people and things that had shaped his life than she wanted to know.

She knew little about art and was helpless to explain why the paintings at the McClure house had come alive for her, told their story so explicitly and overpowered her emotionally with their impact. She did not have the education or the insight to react that way, she told herself. Yes, she knew Dan McClure now, better than many women might know a man in a lifetime of living with him. This intimate knowledge of him, at once attracted her and repelled her, comforted and frightened her.

As the gelding approached the crest of the hill, she nudged him forward, and as they climbed onto the solid footing of the rocky ridge, a bolt of lightning flashed and illuminated the hills for a paralyzing instant. The horse reared, and as Megan yanked at the reins to bring him under control, she caught a glimpse of the rider not more than fifty feet down the trail. The sombrero. The white stallion. It was one of Dunkirk's men. The one they called the Pistolero.

Reflexively, she grabbed for her rifle before she remembered she had borrowed Dan's saddle and had left the Winchester under the seat of the buckboard. A damn greenhorn stunt. She wheeled the horse to her right when the rider's pistol cracked and drove a bullet into the gelding's neck. The horse stumbled to its knees and pitched her over its head, and she somersaulted helplessly over the ridge before slamming back-down on the rain-slicked slope. Winded, she tried to get up, but her feet slipped out from under her and she vaulted forward again, first rolling and then sliding down the incline past the gunman who leveled two hurried shots at her as she tumbled by.

The base of a sturdy ponderosa stopped her downward slide abruptly, and she lay there sprawled against the tree for a moment, dazed and hurting before she looked back up the slope. The rider had ascended the ridge and dismounted. Her instinct was to get up and run, but she froze when she realized that he could not see her through the curtain of rain and pine.

The pistolero—Mendosa, she thought his name was—paced the ridge, his gray silhouette blurry against an almost equally gray sky, like a sentry walking his post on the parapet of a fort. A silent spider web of lightning suddenly lit up the sky again, and he spotted her. His holstered six-gun sprung into his hand. She dodged away just as the bullet thudded against the tree, spitting wood. She dived behind the tree then surrendered to the slippery footing, continuing her downhill journey, riding the steep, rugged slope like a log down a sluice. Finally, as the incline tapered off, she struggled to her feet and paused to catch her breath. She had been too close to the Pistolero. He would know that she had recognized him, and he would not abandon the hunt. He would be working his way down the trail now, knowing she could not scale the greasy slope, confident she would have to stay with the low country. She was on Dan McClure's side of the ridge. She had only to make it to Dan's place not more than a mile away, but a long, and painstakingly slow mile.

She nearly made it to Dan's house when she spied the rider again. He had outsmarted her, guessing where she would be headed, and he was now positioned at one corner of the corral, perhaps one hundred feet from the front porch of the house. He had a rifle cradled in his arms now and was waiting. She could make it very easy for him if she would oblige and make a dash for Dan's door. He would bring her down with a single shot and when Dan opened the door to check out the commotion, the Pistolero would finish the job he had probably botched last time.

There was no way she could reach the house undetected, and the Pistolero had her scent now. There was not a chance he would ride away without making a move. If she tried to wait him out, he would eventually approach the house, perhaps murder Dan. No, one way or another, she would have to bring the pot to a boil.

She crouched down, surveying the scene before her. She dropped to her belly and began to worm her way through the ponderosa break that sheltered the north and west approach to the ranch buildings. She stopped at the edge of the clearing and studied the terrain again. She had a perfect sighting on Mendosa leaning against the corral fence not more than a hundred feet southeast. If she had her Winchester, rain or no rain, she could bring him down with a single shot. But she did not have it.

The house was about fifty feet due east from where she lay, and it fronted to the south where its only windows were set. She could not get to the house without revealing herself to Mendosa.

What if she called out? Would Dan hear her? With the hammering of the rain against the house, it seemed unlikely. If she could lure the gunman away somehow and then circle around and make a dash for the house. Yes, that was her best bet, her only bet if she was not going to run out on Dan McClure, and she had already decided she was not.

She lifted herself up slowly from the ground and inched in behind the thick ponderosa so she was at least partially hidden from Mendosa. She stood there shivering, colder than she could remember even in the depths of a Pine Ridge winter. Her clothes were soupy wet and her arms and the front of her poncho slimy with mud. A wave of nausea swept over her and she knew her strength was ebbing.

"Mendosa!" she called. "I'm over here." She peeked around the tree trunk and saw his head jerk upright, probing the air like a bird dog trying to pick up the scent. He had heard her, but he did not see her. "I've got a bead on you, Mendosa. Drop your gun!" she said, knowing even as she said it that her ruse was doomed to failure.

He swung toward her, his rifle poised in steady hands, and she knew that he had her position in focus. He took several tentative steps in her direction and then stopped, watching and waiting.

She whirled and broke for the timber, clambering for higher, rockier ground, hoping that the gunman's greater bulk would make him less sure-footed. She slipped and tumbled to her knees, and as she caught her breath, she glanced back over her shoulder. The big man had narrowed the gap between them. It would take a miracle for her to escape him now. But she raised herself up and lurched forward, digging her booted heels into the mushy earth as she angled up the rise. Searing pain shot through her chest with each breath, and her temples throbbed until she thought her head would burst. She weaved through the maze of ponderosa, crashing against an unyielding tree trunk, pushing away and staggering on. She hesitated as she maneuvered around a sandstone outcropping that blocked her path, and it was then that her ears caught the sucking of the mud behind her, and she could sense that he was charging like a grizzly for its kill. Even before she felt the thick branch of an arm close across her neck, she knew it was over, that he had her, and she had come face to face with death.

He flung her to the earth, and she collapsed there, stunned, groping in the mud, her mind foggy. Groggily, she turned over and raised herself up on one elbow, shielding her eyes with her hand as she tried to ward off the fierce rain that pelted her face. She could barely make out the blurry mass of the man who towered over her, leering and triumphant.

"Bitch," he snarled. "God damn bitch. You gave me a chase. If I had the time, you'd pay me for your trouble. Pay me like the puta you are."

She struggled futilely like an injured bird to get up, until the gunman's booted foot smashed into her cheekbone and slammed her head against a protruding ragged chunk of granite. She looked up at the fuzzy outline of his rifle aimed to fire, before her vision faded, and she found herself looking into two black, empty tunnels. Panic gripped her for only a moment when she realized she could not see. Exhausted, she surrendered to her fate and fell back, strangely unafraid, to await the bullet that would end it all.

"Take a good look, sweetheart. I'm the last living thing you'll ever see."

Through the pain that racked her skull, it finally registered in her hazy brain she must be staring at the killer, and he, of course, was not aware that she could not see. *What was he waiting for*, she wondered, lying there limp and motionless like a rag doll, the rain pelting her face like tiny stones.

"Kind of hate to do this," she heard the gunman's voice. "Kinda like shootin' a piece of good horseflesh."

The gun exploded, roaring like thunder in her ears. She felt no pain, only a creeping numbness taking over first her legs and then her arms. The spinning in her head was carrying her away like wheat chaff in a whirlwind. So this is how it was to die.

Chapter 8

STRUGGLING TO MAINTAIN his precarious hold on Megan, Dan leaned his rifle against the wall, shifted the young woman in his arms and carried her to the fireplace where he knelt down and placed her gently on the buffalo hide rug. Her chest rose and fell evenly he observed, but her face, normally dark and lustrous, was bleached white. He turned her face toward the fireplace to catch the flickering light. Her left cheek was raw and swollen, puffed up like a mushroom from her upper jaw to her eye. He probed the injury tentatively, satisfying himself that the jaw was not broken.

Then he spied the sticky crimson that matted the disheveled hair above the ear. With deft fingers, he parted the sable strands and uncovered a gaping wound. It was only a few inches long but ominously deep. Fortunately, it seemed to be clotting. It needed attention but could wait.

What troubled him most was the deepness of her sleep. There was not the lightest fluttering of an eyelash, not the faintest moan from her throat, not the least twitch of a muscle. But for the steady rhythm of her breathing, she might have been a model from sculptor's wax. He resolved that whoever had been responsible, whether Dunkirk or someone else, would answer for it.

He got up and started rummaging through the trunk where he stashed his meager wardrobe and momentarily retrieved a faded red union suit. He snatched up two flannel shirts, returned to Megan's side and yanked off her mud-caked boots and soggy woolen socks. Then he removed her shirt and trousers and hesitated only a moment before slipping off her undergarments.

He dried her off quickly and maneuvered her legs and arms into the red flannel. She could almost turn around inside his long johns, Dan thought, but they would keep her warm.

He shoved his cot next to the fireplace and hoisted her off the floor, carefully placing her on the mattress. After covering her with a wool blanket, he was satisfied he had done all he could to make her comfortable, not that she would know the difference in her present state, he thought, but her body should and, hopefully, it would respond.

Next, he washed her face, dabbing tenderly at her puffy cheek which was showing the first traces of blue and purple now. He sponged the sticky blood and mud from the hair that was pasted around the awesome gash above her ear, and as he did so, fresh blood began to trickle from the wound again. It would have to be closed, he decided.

He found his straight-edge razor and came up with a three-inch needle and some tough cord he used for lacing leather. He would have preferred something more refined, but this would have to do. He sliced the hair around the wound away in hunks, and then shaved her scalp bare about three inches on each side of the wound. In a matter of minutes he had adeptly closed the wound with a half-dozen crisscross stitches. That finished, he pulled a chair up beside the bed and, with a deep sigh, dropped onto it. He sat there basking in the warmth of the fire, his neck and shoulders aching, his own healing wounds suddenly throbbing and hurting. He gazed at her sallow, peaceful face, helpless to do more, knowing there was nothing left but the vigil, the wait, to see which way her condition turned.

Damn, if he had insisted that she stay the night or if he had accompanied her back to the Bar G. Of course, she would not have consented to either. He had never seen such a headstrong woman. But who would have dreamed someone would have been stalking the ranch in a storm like this one. Could he or anyone else ever sleep with peace of mind with men like that riding the Pine Ridge? My God, it was 1882, only five years since Custer had met his Maker at the Little Big Horn. A Sioux raid, although unlikely these days, was a risk a man assumed when he set his roots in Pine Ridge. But this murderer was not Sioux: he was white. Dan had not anticipated a war on this front when he purchased the ranch from Ike Hanson.

He thought of the gunslinger he had left sprawled in the mud, stone dead, hands clutched at the bleeding cavern in his chest as if in death trying to dam up the scarlet river that escaped between his fingers.

He glanced over at the Sharps rifle that leaned against the wall. A souvenir of army days. He had snatched it up when he had heard the muffled voices outside because it was handy. The Sharps could bring down a bull buffalo at a hundred yards. What it did to a man at ten, he did not like to think about.

But he had had no choice, he reminded himself. The gunman's own rifle had been aimed at Megan Grant's head when Dan had burst upon the scene. The man had been facing Dan when he broke out of the trees, but he had been so absorbed in finishing off his victim, he had never seen him, and Dan's instincts had told him it was not a time for granting quarter. He had squeezed the trigger of the Sharps, and he winced now at the memory of its recoil against his shoulder in the same instant that the bullet had lifted the man upright and driven him backward with cannon like force before dropping him in the mud. A glance at the fallen gunman had satisfied Dan that the man was beyond help.

Seeing she was unconscious, Dan had scooped Megan up in his arms and trudged back down the hillside for the sanctuary of the ranch house.

Dan's eyes drifted shut and then blinked open, the hair on the back of his neck bristling at the sound of footsteps on the creaking porch. He bolted out of his chair and grabbed the Sharps just as someone rapped harshly on the oak door.

"It's me, Dan," came the familiar raspy voice.

Dan lifted the latch and opened the door. "Come on in, Sol."

"I'm lookin' for Meggie," the grizzled man said. "She ain't come home yet. I came upon your horse over on the ridge. Somebody shot him. I figured maybe Meggie—" Then the old man saw Megan, and he whipped off his hat and hobbled over to her bedside. His face, ruddy from the wet and cold, turned ashen as he stared at Megan's quiet form. He looked up questioningly at Dan.

"I don't know how bad she is, Sol. It's been several hours since I found her. Her face looks bad, I know, but I think it's the gash above her ear that's causing the trouble. Either the man struck her, or she hit her head when she fell. I stitched the wound shut the best I could, but she must have taken quite a blow. She hasn't moved since I brought her here."

"Man . . . what man?"

"I don't know who he was. Big, solid-looking man with kind of a hawk nose. Dark. Wore a Plainsman hat. From what you say, he must have taken a shot at Megan up on the ridge and killed the horse." He shook his head in disbelief. "She must have come all the way back here on foot. Anyway, I thought I heard a voice outside earlier. I suspected it was my imagination, but I went to the window to take a look, and I saw the big man heading across the ranch yard toward the timber on the west side of the house. He had a rifle in his hand, so I figured I'd better check things out. Damn glad I did. He was getting ready to put a bullet in Megan just as I got there."

"What happened to him?"

"He's dead. I left him where he fell. Maybe you'll know who he is. You can take a look in the morning."

"Sounds like Rafael Mendosa. He wears a Plainsman. He's one of Dunkirk's hired guns. My guess is he was headed to your place and saw a chance to kill two flies with one swat."

"I'm still skeptical, Sol. I can't believe anyone would kill for a piece of land. But if this man works for Dunkirk, like you say he does, I'll see that he gets back to his boss. I'll deliver him personally."

Sol grunted. "Do what you want, young fellar. I don't give a good goddamn anymore." He nodded toward Megan. "You seem to know a little somethin' about doctoring. What do you think?"

"All we can do is wait. I don't know any more than you do. I dealt with wounded soldiers when I was in the field because I had to, and I watched the post surgeon at Camp Robinson and picked up a few things. I've seen people lie unconscious for several days and then wake up bright and alert like nothing had ever happened."

"I've been around some, too," Sol said, his voice cracking. "but I've seen more than one that never woke up."

Dan placed a comforting hand on Sol's shoulder. "She'll wake up, Sol, I know she will. Bed down here tonight, and we'll wait this out together."

"I wasn't planning on going no place," Sol said. "I'll put my horse up in your barn. While I'm out, I'll see if I can round up that dead jasper's mount."

After Sol returned from putting up the horses, Dan threw some blankets on the floor. He was not as strong yet as he thought. The exhaustion was overpowering him and his strength was draining away like sand through an hourglass. He felt light-headed and slightly nauseous and knew that if he didn't get rest, he would be flat on his back in a matter of minutes.

Sol had taken up the vigil at Megan's bedside, and as Dan stretched out on the floor, the old man said, "Get some shut eye, young fellar. I'll wake you to spell me later."

"Let me know if she starts to come out of it," Dan said.

"I will, son."

Dan curled up, his hip and shoulder shifting futilely in an attempt to find a soft spot on the hardwood floor. But Dan was too tired to fret about it much. He looked up at the old man who kept his watch at Megan's bedside, a gnarled hand resting on her lifeless arm, his weary, green eyes fastened on her face. Bleak eyes that reflected deep morose and pain. Those eyes. Where had he seen them before? Had his path crossed with Solomon Pyle's at some other time and place? He always remembered eyes. He thought of them as the windows to the soul. If he painted the eyes right, he had the person right, no matter what other flaws might mar the canvas.

Then he knew. Yes, he had seen those eyes before. He dropped off into a drugged sleep.

* * *

When he woke up, he was greeted by a bright, sun-filled room. The storm had passed. Dan tossed off the blankets and sat up, shaking his head groggily, trying to clear his mind. "Why in the hell didn't you wake me so you could get some rest?"

"I was going to wake you, son," Solomon Pyle said from his station by the bed. "But I wasn't in no state for sleepin' and you was limp as a neck-wrung rooster. You did your job; sitting here was mine."

"How is she?"

"She ain't come around yet, but she's been stirring some."

Dan got up and stepped over beside the bed. Megan was turning her head slowly from side to side, her arms flailing helplessly as Sol pinned her shoulders gently, but firmly against the bed and whispered soothingly like a man might calm a skittish horse. A wave of relief swept over Dan. She was climbing out of it; she was going to pull through.

Suddenly, Megan's body tensed and just as quickly relaxed and her eyes opened. "Sol?" she asked.

"Right here, Meggie," he said touching fingers to her pale cheek.

"Sol," she choked, her eyes jerking wildly without seeming to focus.

"Meggie? What is it, child?"

"I . . . I can't see. Sol, what's wrong with me? Mendosa? Where is he?"

Sol Pyle looked like a man who had been kicked in the balls, Dan thought. Breathless, Dan knelt down beside the bed. "Megan, it's Dan McClure. You're all right. You're in my house. Mendosa's dead. Everything's going to be fine."

Her hands went to her face. Her fingers explored the flesh around her eyes, touching her eyelids as if to confirm that all the parts were there. Her teeth dug into her lower lip and several of the tears she was trying to hold back squeezed out of the corners of her eyes.

"I can't see anything," she cried. "I can't see. I . . . I'm blind."

Dan could see she was on the verge of panic, bravely trying to subdue the fear, the utter terror that had to be overwhelming her. He took her hand in his and drew it away from her face.

"Megan, I know it's easy to say, but don't be afraid. Sol and I are here, and we're not going anyplace."

"I can't help it," she replied, her voice husky. "I'm frightened. More than I've ever been."

"I can understand," Dan said. "You had a blow on the head. Give it time."

"How much time? An hour? A day? A month?"

"I don't know. A few days, maybe."

"What if I can't see then?"

"We'll take you to Fort Robinson and have the post surgeon take a look at you."

"What if he says I won't see again?"

Dan hesitated. Sol looked up at him with glazed eyes. "Then you won't," Dan said, "and you'll have to adjust to it and accept it."

She yanked her hand away. "You cold son-of-a-bitch. You act like I stubbed my toe or something." She curled up in a ball and began to sob pathetically. "I don't want to live if I can't see," she murmured.

"Yes, you do," Dan said, his voice firm. "Now, get hold of yourself."

"Get away from me. Get out of here!" she screamed.

"Meggie, child," Sol said.

"I am not a child," she snapped, choking back tears.

"Then quit acting like one," Dan said.

Sol's face flushed. "Now look here, Dan. We're in your debt for what you done, but there ain't no need to be so damned mean about this."

"There's no debt, Sol. Besides, this would have never happened if Megan hadn't come over to help me out. But she's got to be patient. She doesn't have any other choice. You and I both know the best thing she can do right now is eat and rest."

"Damn you, Dan McClure," Megan said, turning toward Dan, composing herself. "I'm here. You can talk to me. Both of you, quit talking back and forth like I'm deaf or something." She paused while she touched her arms and legs inquisitively. "What am I wearing?"

"My long johns," Dan said.

"I don't remember putting them on."

"You didn't. I did."

"You mean you took my clothes off? Stripped me naked?"

"Well, not entirely. I didn't take off the emerald ring you wear on your right hand." He was pleased to see some color returning to her cheeks now.

"Damn you, Dan McClure. Double damn you. What right did you have to do that?"

"Megan, please, swearing isn't becoming of a lady. And believe me, I didn't have time to notice a thing." And he hadn't at the time. But he found himself now consciously remembering more than Megan would have liked and the memory was a rather pleasant one.

"I suppose now I'll end up in one of your filthy paintings," she said.

"You don't have to worry about that," Dan said. "Not the way you look now. Half bald, your face swollen like a pumpkin. No, I'll pass."

Her eyes, though unseeing, blazed momentarily and swelled up with tears, and he could see her straight, white teeth gritting between slightly parted lips. "I hate you, Dan McClure. I have you to thank for this. I'll never forget that."

She spoke slowly, almost hissing it out. Her words stung, but he had accomplished his purpose. He had lured out the feisty bobcat in her; now she was ready to fight and that's what she would have to do in the days that lay ahead.

Sol sat there motionless, his shoulders slumped, his face skewered up, and a perplexed look in his eyes.

"Sol," Megan said, "I don't want to stay here. Take me home. Now."

"But Meggie, I don't think you're ready to travel."

"I said now. I won't stay another minute in this man's house. If you won't take me, I'll go on my own. You can't hold me here. I'll get out of bed and find my way out somehow. I'll walk home if I have to."

The old man patted her consolingly on the arm. "Now, Meggie, just you calm down."

"All right, old man. You don't believe me?" She lifted herself shakily and sat up in bed. "I'm going home."

Sol shrugged and held out his hands in an empty gesture. He looked up at Dan, his eyes pleading.

"She wants to go home, Sol. I think you'd better take her," Dan said. "Megan?"

She did not reply but sat there on the bed, her lips pursed tight, her arms folded across her chest, as though protecting the small, well-defined breasts that Dan knew lay beneath the woolen underwear.

"I'll make a bargain with you, Megan," Dan continued. "Let me rustle up some breakfast, and we'll all have something to eat. Then I'll help Sol hitch up your buckboard and get you settled in for the ride home. Will you let me do that much?"

She was silent for a moment before she answered. "Doesn't look like I have much choice."

"I'm glad you see it that way," Dan said, and then he turned away to see if he could round up something that would whet her appetite.

Sol helped Megan ease back down on the mattress. Strangely, Dan found himself sorrier for Solomon Pyle than for Megan Grant.

Chapter 9

DAN MCCLURE NUDGED his claybank gelding down the muddy main street of Medicine Hill, Nebraska. He glanced back at the stiff mud-smeared and blood-caked body that was slung across the saddle and tied to the black mare that trailed behind. As they plodded down the street, he tipped his low-brimmed hat from time to time at the curious passers-by who stopped to stare. As he approached the sheriff's office, he reined in his horse and dismounted. His hand came to rest on the butt of the long barreled Army model Colt holstered on his hip, and he wondered absently how it could feel so comfortable there after so long an absence.

He led the horses over to the hitching rail in front of the sheriff's office and hitched them there, before stepping up onto the boardwalk just as the thick, oak door of the jailhouse office swung open and an eel-thin man with a sallow face and black pencil-thin mustache swaggered out. The glittering silver star on the man's leather vest told Dan this was the man he had come to see.

The sheriff stopped and, ignoring Dan for a moment, eyed the dead gunman with what seemed to be only casual interest. He lifted off his Stetson and primped at his neatly trimmed, coal-black hair before repositioning it deliberately on his head. He pulled a small cigar from his shirt pocket, bit off the end, and finally stepped toward Dan. His dark reptilian eyes searched Dan. "Who are you?" the sheriff asked.

"My name's Dan McClure. I live about 15 miles northwest of here."

The sheriff lit his cigar and sucked at it deeply, his eyes meeting Dan's challengingly. He was an imposing and formidable figure, Dan thought, one of the few he had encountered who was taller than himself. His crooked nose, which likely had been broken on some occasion, gave his face a sinister look, and his body appeared loose and quick, like a walking bullwhip. Instinctively, he disliked the man.

"Ike Hanson's place," the sheriff said matter-of-factly. "You're the nester who moved in there."

The sheriff kept in pretty good touch with his territory considering there must have been over three thousand square miles in the county. Too good of touch, maybe.

"I'm not a nester. I bought the place from Hanson. My deed's recorded. I assume you're Keaton."

The sheriff blew out a thick plume of smoke that caught Dan full in the face. The smoke seared his eyes, but Dan did not give the sheriff the satisfaction of flinching.

"Sheriff Keaton. Sheriff Stiles Keaton." He nodded toward the dead man. "Now, suppose you tell me what this is all about."

"This man tried to kill a young woman, Sheriff. He would have if I hadn't gotten there first."

"You killed him?"

"Yes, I did. I had to or he would have killed Megan Grant."

"Grant? Of the Bar G Grants?"

"Yes. He stalked her and beat her senseless. He was going to shoot her when I came along. The way it is, he left her blind. I've got a hunch he's the bushwhacker who put a bullet in me a few weeks back."

"Any witnesses?"

"Nobody saw who shot me. But Miss Grant recognized this man, and she can testify that he was trying to kill her."

"Appears to me there's no need to testify. The man's dead. The law can't do much more to him. And I'll take you at your word you didn't kill him in cold blood . . . for now."

"I left home late yesterday afternoon and spent the night in the timber so I could report this, Sheriff. I wanted to keep my own name clear, but more importantly, I wanted to be sure that somebody looked into this."

"Looked into what?"

"From what the folks at the Grant ranch tell me, you've got a small-scale range war going on in this county, but from what I hear and from what I've seen so far, you're getting damn close to a real blood-letting."

"If folks want to fight, I can't stop them," the sheriff said.

"I don't see why not. At least you can hear out their grievances and try to do something about it."

"What grievances? Hell, mister, you haven't made a lick of sense since you rode up here."

"I'm talking about the small ranchers and their family members who've been killed over the past few years," Dan said. "I'm told you never even rode out to take a look after the killings were reported."

"Nobody could ever come up with witnesses. Hell, you can't do anything without witnesses. Anyway, mister, I don't like the way you're putting things. Are you trying to say I'm not doing my job?"

"I'm just making it clear that I expect you to find out what this is all about or make a damn good try at it."

"And what if I don't?"

"I've already posted a letter to the Nebraska Attorney General, who happens to be a good friend of mine," Dan lied. "I told him what I know and asked him to make some inquiries here."

"I don't take kindly to people going over my head," Stiles Keaton said.

"I don't take kindly to people shooting at me."

"Well, I'll look into it," Keaton said, "but don't push me. I don't like to be pushed."

"What about this man?" Dan asked.

"What about him? He's dead, isn't he? Like I said, what more can I do?"

"You miss my point. I want to know who hired him. Do you know this man?"

"Can't say that I do. Hell, folks are so strung out in this county he could have lived here for years without me seeing him."

"You don't look like the kind of man who would miss anything he wanted to know about, but I won't argue the point. His name's Mendosa. I have reason to think he works for Woodson Dunkirk. The Diamond D. You've heard of the spread?" Dan asked sarcastically. Dan thought he saw a fleeting moment of surprise, or something akin to it, cross the man's eyes.

"I'd be careful about tossing Dunkirk's name around free and loose like that, mister."

"Why, because he might have me killed?"

Keaton's jaw tensed. "Mr. Dunkirk's a fine man. That's not his way. But he carries a lot of weight in these parts, and he's a good man to get along with."

"And you get along with him, is that right, Sheriff?"

"Look, mister, I said I don't like to be pushed, and in about two shakes, I'm going to rub your nose in that shit that's running out of your mouth."

He decided he had pressed the sheriff beyond prudence, but he had accomplished what he had set out to do. He had confirmed what Sol and Megan had told him: that Sheriff Keaton was uncooperative and hostile, if not on Dunkirk's payroll. And the latter was a distinct possibility. But he had put the sheriff on guard, and if Keaton thought the Attorney General might be breathing down his neck, perhaps he would be a little more careful. Maybe he'd press Dunkirk to pull in his horns for a spell. And perhaps it would be wise to actually write a letter to the Attorney General. The Pine Ridge was a powder keg with a short fuse, and it appeared that the small ranchers had nobody to turn to for help.

"What about this man . . . Mendosa?" Dan asked. "What shall I do with him?"

"I don't have any use for him," the sheriff said. "I'd say it's your shit: cover it up."

"You won't see to having him buried?"

"Nope."

"Do you want to know more about what happened out at my place?"

"Not especially. I told you, mister, I'll look into it on my own. If I need something more from you, I'll be in touch. Now, why don't you get this corpse off the street?" He cast his eyes skyward. "That sun's going to be warming things up, and your friend here's getting ripe enough already. He'll be drawin' out the early flies before the afternoon's out. If I was you, I'd head out of town and bury him up the road a ways. Then I'd skedaddle back to that place you're nesting on, pack my duds, and look for a better fishing hole someplace else."

Dan tipped his hat with exaggerated politeness, turned away, and ambled over to the horses. He untied the reins and moved to the claybank's side, feeling the sheriff's eyes boring into his back all the while. He grasped the saddle horn, stepped into the stirrup, and swung into the saddle. He looked down at the sheriff. "Sheriff," he said, "you say you don't like to be pushed. I'm going to tell you something. It seems like we've got something in common. I don't like to be pushed either. But if somebody pushes me, I don't push back. I hit back. And I hit hard."

"I'll tell you something, Mr. . . . McClure, isn't it? This job was starting to bore me until you came along. I was even thinking I might move on west a little further, maybe Wyoming, Montana, where things are a little livelier. But I think I'll stick around a spell now. I've got a feeling you'll make things a little more interesting. A challenge. That's what I think you might be: a challenge. You and me, we just might have to see who's going to be bull of the herd."

"I'll watch my back closer from now on," Dan said, as he reined his horse away from the hitching rail. "And by the way, since nobody will claim this stray dog, I think I'll just run him out to the Diamond D and see if he's got an owner out there. Everybody tells me how important this Mr. Dunkirk is. The most powerful man in the county, they say. Maybe in this half of the state. He sounds like the kind of man I should get to know." Dan shot a final glance at Keaton.

The sheriff was standing there in the shadows of the portico. His right arm was hanging limply, within easy grasp of the pearl-handled revolver that hung low on his hip. Dan guessed it was taking all the willpower Stiles Keaton could muster to keep that hand from groping for the gun right now. He had made an enemy this day, and looking back, he had done it with an arrogance and bravado that had not been necessary. He could have learned everything he wanted without baiting the sheriff to such anger, but there was something in the man that stirred emotions he had thought long since dead. He had put hate and killing aside for love and the gentle pursuit of art. But there was no doubt in his mind now that he could still kill. The thought saddened him.

Chapter 10

DAN HAD NO trouble finding the Diamond D. The road was wide and smooth, not wagon-rutted or half over-grown by brush like most of the county roads. Somebody, either Dunkirk or the county officials, kept the road from Medicine Hill to the Diamond D in top shape.

The Diamond D ranch headquarters was some five miles up the valley and then angled north and west from Medicine Hill, but the well-built road bed connected the ranch to the town like an umbilical cord anchored a baby to its mother, Dan thought. However, he could not say for sure whether the town was the mother of the ranch or the ranch the mother of the town. He was beginning to see why the small ranchers did not look to Medicine Hill to take up any grievances against Woodson Dunkirk.

As he cantered the horses westward, Dan observed that the trees were becoming sparser and that the valley widened and flattened into a plain carpeted with tough, fine-stemmed buffalo grass that, in spite of the soaking rain, had only begun to shuck the crisp, brown residue of winter. But Dan knew that by August, the silvery green grass, after a month of drought and heavy pasturage, would glisten with life after other less hardy grasses had shriveled away and been stomped into the Pine Ridge dust.

Dan slowed the gelding and surveyed the seemingly endless sea of grass spread out before him. At the far end of the open meadows, just before they gave way to the rolling foothills that climbed into the Pine Ridge, he could make out the gray outline of ranch buildings. He nudged his horse ahead, and as he drew closer to the main gate of the Diamond D, he caught sight of the gleaming strands of newly strung barbed wire that stretched out from both sides of the swinging pinewood gate that blocked the road. The approach to the ranch headquarters reminded Dan of a military post, and there was even a sentry, a range cowboy with a rifle cradled in his arms, leaning lazily against the thick cedar post that anchored the heavy gate in a casual manner, belying the intense scrutiny his eyes were giving the approaching rider and the cargo that trailed behind.

Beyond the gate, perhaps a half mile down the road, Dan could identify the barns and sheds and bunk houses of the sprawling Diamond D ranch complex. And dominating it all, rising like a towering monument from the prairie, stood a white, pillared Georgian mansion. It didn't fit. A house like that didn't belong in the West. Somehow—he could not explain why—the house seemed ugly and offensive in this setting, an affront to the hard-working, self-sacrificing people who were settling and building the West. Dan did not begrudge a man his material rewards. In his own way, he supposed, although not obsessed by it, he too desired a measure of wealth and fame. But the mansion flaunted it. Here it struck Dan like an obscene gesture.

"Hold up there, mister," came the cowboy's voice as Dan rode up to the gate. The man straightened up and pushed up the brim of his hat, all the while looking up at Dan with challenging eyes. He nodded toward the body that was slung over the mare. "Where'd you find Mendosa?"

So the cowboy knew the gunslinger, although he did not appear shocked or saddened by the man's death. "I take it you know the man," Dan said.

The cowboy's Winchester shifted in his hands, and he turned back to Dan, his look guarded. "Maybe. Maybe not."

This man was no gunman, Dan decided; he was a cowhand who would much rather be punching cows right now than confronting a stranger bearing a corpse. The heavy stubble in his cheeks, at first glance, had made him seem older, but now Dan realized that the guard was a young man not far into his twenties. He persisted. "Did this man work for the Diamond D?"

"I wouldn't know," the cowhand said sullenly. "This is a big ranch."

"You knew his name."

"I seen him around."

"Where?"

The cowboy's face flushed. "Now see here, mister, I ain't standin' out here to answer your damn fool questions. You'll answer mine if you're fixin' to go through that gate. Now, like I said before, where'd you find this fella?"

"I didn't. He found me, and I killed him. I was told he worked for Dunkirk, so I thought the least the Diamond D could do would be to see to his burial. I came to leave him with Mr. Dunkirk."

The cowboy edged back toward the gate, his grip tightening on the rifle. "No, mister, I don't think so. I don't think Mr. Dunkirk would take kindly to your stopping by."

"That doesn't matter. I came a long way. I expect to see him anyway." Dan's revolver slid into his hand and was pointed at the cowhand's chest before the latter could lift his rifle. "Put your gun down, friend," Dan said. "I don't pull my gun unless I'm ready to use it. There's no sense in a young man like you ending up like Mendosa." Dan saw the man's hand inching its way up the rifle stock toward the trigger. The hammer on Dan's pistol clicked ominously as he pulled it back. "Don't do it, kid. Don't be a jackass." The young man's fingers relaxed their grip, and the rifle dropped at his feet. "Now your six-gun. Just take hold of it, and let it out of your holster, slow and easy." The cowboy obeyed and dropped it on the ground beside the rifle. Dan waved his pistol toward the buckskin mare that was tied to a fence post a short distance away. "Now, why don't you get your horse, and take me up to that big white house? You can give me a proper introduction."

The man kicked at the dirt and moved for the horse. "You just bought yourself a heap o' trouble, mister. Mr. Dunkirk don't like uninvited guests. He'll have the hide stripped right off your ass for this. You just wait and see."

"I'll wait," Dan said, "and I'll see. Now saddle up."

Chapter 11

A S THEY DISMOUNTED in front of the Dunkirk mansion, a lanky man with a full blond beard stepped out from under a mammoth cottonwood where he had been hidden in the shadows. He wore his six-gun low on the hip, Dan noted, and he walked with a self-assured stride that said he was no ordinary cowhand, and the spotless buckskin jacket and tailored trousers and shiny boots confirmed that the man had not spent this day, nor many others, roping steers and branding calves.

"Trouble, Levi?" the man asked as he walked up to the horses, his steel gray eyes locked on the blanket-wrapped bundle.

"This jasper got the drop on me, Clay. Says he wants to see Mr. Dunkirk."

The blond man gazed at the body, ignoring Dan's presence. "I'll go talk to Mr. Dunkirk," he said. "I'll see what he says."

He wheeled without so much as a glance at Dan and headed toward the massive double doors of the Dunkirk home. Dan tied his horses at two of the hitching posts that formed a boundary between the dusty ranch yard and the well-manicured front lawn of the mansion.

"Tell me, Levi," Dan said, his tone friendly as he saw the door close behind the blond man. "Is he Mr. Dunkirk's foreman?"

Levi eyed Dan suspiciously and scratched the stubble on his chin, apparently deciding he wasn't all that mad. "Hell, no," he said, "Mr. Dunkirk's got working foremen on his ranches. Clay Sutherly's above that kind of work."

Dan did not miss the tinge of sarcasm in the cowboy's voice. "Clay Sutherly's what Mr. Dunkirk calls his manager," Levi continued. "Kind of a right-hand man. He looks after everything, including the old man's daughter."

"I see."

"Mister, you don't seem like such a bad sort. Let me put it plain, then I'm going to shut up. Clay Sutherly is as cold as a banker's heart, and he looks to own the Diamond D someday. His bed roll's laid out in the big house already, and when he and Miss Dunkirk marry up in the fall, he's got his future made. He sees Mr. Dunkirk's business as his business, and if anybody gets in the way, he'll stomp 'em like a dung beetle, with just as much worry about it. Know what I'm sayin'? He's a man to watch out for. Stay clear out of his way."

The door opened and Sutherly stepped out. He stood there for a moment, studying Dan, a scowl etched on his angular face. Dan stared back, doing his own sizing up of the ranch manager. Sutherly was of average height; his bearing made him appear larger. Dan supposed that women might find the man ruggedly handsome and might well be attracted to the self-assurance and confidence he obviously carried, but on Dan's part, his impulsive judgment was that love, other than self, was an emotion that would run very shallow in Clay Sutherly.

"What's your name, mister?" Sutherly said from his position in front of the door some twenty-five feet away.

"McClure. Dan McClure."

Sutherly gave a slight nod, as if confirming what he already knew. "Levi said you wanted to see Mr. Dunkirk. What's your business?"

"I prefer to tell Mr. Dunkirk."

"I speak for Mr. Dunkirk."

"Maybe. But I don't want you to listen for him. I own Ike Hanson's place. I think Mr. Dunkirk will want to hear what I have to say."

"Mr. Dunkirk is a busy man. He doesn't have much time for palaver. But he'll talk to you for a few minutes. You'll have to make it quick. You can come in the house, but leave your gun belt on your horse."

"Are you leaving yours outside?" Dan asked. Sutherly glared back. "Then I'll wear mine," Dan said, moving toward the house, and as soon as the words slipped out, he chastised himself for the unnecessary display of bravado. That was the second time today he had let his tongue override his good sense. He should know better.

Sutherly led Dan through the doors which opened into a cavernous foyer with a giant glittering crystal chandelier and a double staircase that climbed to the second floor balcony. The room, no doubt, doubled as a ballroom when the Dunkirks entertained, and Dan conceded he had never seen a room so stunning. And he had been in many splendid homes when he and Larisa had lived in the East for a brief period following their marriage when, like the dutiful son-in-law he could not be, he had filled a chair as vice president in her industrialist father's munitions firm. Larisa's family was old money in Boston, going back to pre-Revolutionary days, and they moved in elite circles. But a visit to the Dunkirk home would have made them feel like paupers.

They stood there for a moment while Dan took in the room, and he had a feeling that Sutherly's pause here was his way of preparing Dan for the audience with the king. Dan studied the room with an artist's eyes, concluding quickly that its accouterments, individually, were elegant and beautiful and, at the same time, out of place and tasteless in their setting.

Suddenly, his heart hammered and his pulse raced when he looked up and saw the young woman standing on the balcony at the top of the winding stairway, her hair gleaming and golden as a western sunrise, flowing over her shoulders like spun silk. For a fleeting moment, he thought he saw Larisa standing there—or her ghost.

The woman stared back at him, her deep blue eyes inquisitive. She stepped slowly down the staircase, watching him all the way. It was her poise, Dan thought, her almost regal bearing that reminded him of Larisa, for as she drew closer he realized that aside from the coloring of her hair and the fairness of her skin, her resemblance to Larisa was slight.

The woman who approached him was statuesque, and although slender, quite voluptuous, with ample cleavage threatening to spill over the top of her dress. Larisa had been petite, almost frail. He knew before she spoke a word that this woman would be forward and unconstrained, if not downright brash. Larisa had been quiet, reserved, and soft-spoken.

She stepped up to him, studying him, her lips parting in an amused smile. "Who are you?" she asked.

Her manner was cordial enough in spite of her directness. "My name's Dan McClure."

"I'm Elizabeth Dunkirk," she said. "You may call me Liz. My, you're a tall man and quite handsome, too."

"Thank you. And you're quite beautiful."

"This man came to see your father, Elizabeth," Sutherly said. "He's waiting in the study, and you know he doesn't like to be kept waiting."

In his enchantment with Elizabeth Dunkirk, Dan had been oblivious to Clay Sutherly's presence in the room, and a glance at the man's flushed face and stormy eyes told him that Sutherly was enraged. That pleased Dan.

"I won't be but a moment, Clay," Elizabeth Dunkirk said. "Besides, you're just trying to impress Mr. McClure. Daddy's not all that busy, and I doubt if Mr. McClure impresses all that easily. Do you live in the Pine Ridge, Mr. McClure?"

"Yes, about five miles west of here."

"You're a rancher then?"

"I don't make my living at ranching, but I own a small ranch. I bought it recently from Mr. Hanson."

"Oh, the Ike Hanson ranch. I know the place. I've been there. It's very scenic. An idyllic setting. My father tried to buy the ranch from Mr. Hanson for years. He wants to own it very badly."

"So I've been told."

"I'm glad you purchased it, Mr. McClure."

"Dan."

"Very well, Dan. I think you will present an interesting challenge for my father. But you say you don't make your living as a rancher. May I ask what you do?"

"I'm a painter."

"You mean an artist?"

"Yes."

"How interesting. I visited galleries when I was at school in the East. I thought it would be fascinating to know a painter. I always wanted to watch an artist paint. Do you ever let anyone watch you?"

"It depends on what I'm painting. I have my quirks, I guess. I can't let anyone see a portrait until it's finished, but I don't mind letting someone watch while I work a landscape."

"Could I see your paintings sometime? Do you suppose I might watch you paint? I'd be quiet as a mouse."

"Certainly. Drop by my ranch sometime. I'd be delighted to show you my work."

He liked Elizabeth Dunkirk. If Woodson Dunkirk could sire a daughter like that, Dan found it hard to believe that he could be all bad. And still, he knew his judgment about people was not infallible. For some reason, he often did not seem to know them till he tried to paint them.

"Elizabeth," Sutherly said, "I think you'd better excuse Mr. McClure now."

"Oh, very well, Clay. You can be such a bore." She gave an exaggerated curtsey. "Good day, Dan. I can't wait to see your paintings."

She whirled and hurried out the room, leaving behind the intoxicating image of the swell of her generous bosom framed by the daring indigo dress that Dan guessed would have scandalized most of the Pine Ridge matrons. He hoped Elizabeth Dunkirk was sincere when she said she would be dropping by to see his paintings.

"Follow me," Sutherly snapped, jolting Dan back to the purpose of his mission.

Dan trailed the man down the hallway that led away from the foyer. At the end of the hall, Sutherly paused at an ornately carved oak door and rapped softly. "Come in, Clay," came a strong, precise voice from within. Sutherly opened the door and led Dan into a spacious room with book-lined walls and leather-covered chairs.

The room was dominated by a huge mahogany desk and, almost dwarfed behind it, sat a pale, wizened man with chalk-white hair. He sat stiff-backed with his elbows resting on the arms of the chair and his bony fingers interlaced in front of him, staring at Dan with porcine eyes, hidden behind layered folds of flesh. This had to be Woodson Dunkirk, but the man was a far cry from the image Dan had conjured up of him. This frail old man was the scourge of Pine Ridge? My God, he had to be well into his seventies, and he looked every bit of it.

Without standing or even shifting in his chair, the old man spoke in a commanding, unwavering voice that did not fit his body. "Mr. McClure, I am told that you insist upon speaking with me."

"That's right, if you're Mr. Dunkirk."

"I am." The old man nodded at a chair in front of the desk. "You may sit down if you wish."

Dan took the chair and Sutherly sank into an overstuffed chair off to one side. "I had hoped to talk with you privately, Mr. Dunkirk," Dan said.

"Mr. Sutherly can hear anything you have to say to me," Dunkirk said.

Dan decided not to press the issue for the moment. "All right, I'll get right to the point, Mr. Dunkirk. I killed a man over at my place. I have been told his name was Mendosa and that he rode for the Diamond D."

The old man's brow wrinkled. "Mendosa?" He turned to Sutherly. "Do we have a Mendosa on our payroll?"

"No, Mr. Dunkirk, this man heard wrong. We don't have anybody with that handle working here."

Dunkirk turned back to Dan. "I'm afraid you were mistaken, Mr. McClure. Now, if that was the only purpose of your visit—"

"Mr. Dunkirk, there's a body outside on one of my horses. I intend to dump it here on your ranch yard. I'm satisfied that the man had some connection with the Diamond D. I also have reason to believe you are interested in acquiring my ranch." Dan started to rise. "Now, if you don't want to talk about these things, fine. I'll unload Mr. Mendosa and be on my way."

Dunkirk waved Dan back in his chair. "Now, don't be hasty, Mr. McClure. It can't do any harm to talk about this."

He had taken the bait. Dunkirk's eyes had brightened noticeably at the mention of the ranch.

"As I said before, Mr. Dunkirk, I'd like to speak to you privately. I don't think I have anything else to say in Mr. Sutherly's presence."

The old man leaned forward in his chair, his eyes thoughtful, and after a moment of silence, he said, "Clay, why don't you tend to this man Mendosa. The poor devil's entitled to a burial no matter who he is. Have some of the boys plant him in the drifter's plot. We can at least relieve our neighbor here of that concern."

The muscles in Sutherly's neck tightened and his face grew scarlet. "Mr. Dunkirk, this man is carrying a gun."

"Now, Clay," Dunkirk chided, "Mr. McClure hardly seems the kind to use his gun imprudently. I don't think he came here to kill me. Not this visit anyway," he said meaningfully. "I'll chat with Mr. McClure a bit. Now, I would consider it a favor if you would look to the disposition of Mr. Mendosa."

Sutherly glowered at Dan a moment, and Dan could see that the man was a simmering volcano. Then Sutherly lifted himself out of the chair and stalked out of the room, slamming the door behind him.

"You'll have to excuse Clay," Dunkirk said, "he's somewhat on the temperamental side. But don't underestimate him. He's very shrewd and, I might say, intensely loyal. Of course, you must pay a certain price for his kind of loyalty," Dunkirk said musingly. "But you didn't come here to talk about Mr. Sutherly, so I suggest we pursue the conversation we started. About the sale of your ranch?"

"We were talking about Mr. Mendosa and your interest in my ranch," Dan corrected.

"Very well."

"Mr. Dunkirk, Mendosa tried to kill a young woman, Megan Grant. He didn't quite get the job done, but he left her blind. This happened on my ranch, and I have a hunch that he'd come to finish a job he'd left undone a few weeks earlier."

"I'm afraid I don't understand. Please don't speak in riddles, Mr. McClure. I don't like that." Dunkirk was a tough old bird. He would not be easily intimidated. "I was bushwhacked in my ranch yard several weeks ago. Shot in the back. If Megan Grant and her foreman, Sol Pyle, hadn't come along, I wouldn't be here right now."

"That's terribly unfortunate," Dunkirk said matter-of-factly.

Dan could not tell whether it was unfortunate he had been shot, or unfortunate that Megan and Sol had come to his assistance.

"Yes, it is too bad because I don't like violence. I came to the Pine Ridge to paint. I was looking for peace here. I want to get along with my neighbors. But I am capable of violence, Mr. Dunkirk. Mendosa found out the hard way."

"So it would seem."

"I came here, Mr. Dunkirk, because I've almost been persuaded that Mendosa was hired by the Diamond D to kill me."

Dunkirk seemed unperturbed. "You're not making any sense, young man. Why, for whatever reason, would I want to have you killed?"

"I suppose it would make it easier for you to acquire my ranch. The administrator of my estate would no doubt put it on the market, or if nobody claimed it, you could just move in."

"Mr. McClure, need I remind you that your ranch is no more than a garden plot in comparison to my land holdings."

"I'm aware of that. But I've also been trained as an engineer, and I've been informed that my ranch is the key to the water supply for a sizable amount of your grazing land. Besides, if you could acquire my ranch and the Bar G, you'd be able to tie a big part of our land into a single unit. I can see the possibilities. I can understand why you might want my ranch and the Bar G, but I can't see why you'd kill for it."

"Are you accusing me, Mr. McClure?"

"Not yet, but there are a lot of small ranchers who are, I'm told. Most of the ranchers around here live on islands in the middle of the Diamond D, and their owners seem to think it's just a matter of time before they're swallowed up by your operation."

"It's a free country. They don't have to sell."

"Apparently a lot of people have died because they didn't."

"Perhaps you should consider the source of your information. I wouldn't look upon the Bar G as reliable in that regard."

"Why not?"

"Ben Grant harbored a grudge against me for years before he died. I knew Ben in his Texas days. I'll wager Solomon Pyle didn't tell you that, did he, Mr. McClure?"

"No, I wasn't aware of it."

"Ben Grant was my foreman in the mid fifties. He had a few acres of his own on the side. He was too ambitious a man to content himself with a lifetime of running someone else's ranch. I knew that. He was a damn good foreman and I was glad to have him for as long as he would stay. But he was also a dyed-in-the-wool Johnny Reb, and I was a strong Union man. A man's entitled to his own opinion, and I didn't hold it against him . . . until the Rebs in our community started taking the notion that my cows and my ranch were fair game because they were Union bred and owned. I lost half my herd to neighboring ranchers who just rode in and ran off with the cows in broad daylight, just like they owned them. The sheriff was Reb and he wouldn't do anything about it. Grant wasn't any help. He refused to do anything to track down the rustlers or get my cattle back. I always figured he was in on it. Probably got his own cow herd started with mine as seed stock. Anyway, I fired him. I sent him and his wife packing. We had words before he left. He said he'd see me and my kind run out of Texas."

"He was right," Dunkirk continued. "He, or at least his kind of people ran off most of the rest of my herd over the next several years. Burned out my line shacks and barns. Scared off my hands after they killed a few. Destroyed one of the finest ranches in all of Texas. Finally, one evening in '59, just before the war broke out, I came home after a trip to town to make one last plea for help from the law, and I found my home, a magnificent mansion, precisely like this one incidentally, in flames. My servants, my ranch hands, everybody, had deserted the place, except two. My wife had stayed behind. She lay in the yard, stripped naked and bloodied. She'd been raped, God knows how many times, before some bastard cut her throat. And my little girl, not yet three years old, sat on the ground beside my wife, clutching her mother's dead hand while she screamed like nothing I ever heard before or since. Let me tell you, McClure, something like that tears a man's guts out. I was nearly fifty-five years old and everything I'd built and loved was in shambles."

The old man had disarmed him, Dan conceded. With the telling of his own sad tale, Dunkirk had put him on the defensive.

Woodson Dunkirk went on. "But I'm a practical man, and I saw the handwriting on the wall. I was fighting a losing battle in Texas. I sold my holdings for little of nothing and took my daughter north. Fortunately, I had made investments outside of ranching, and I still had a rather healthy stake to start again. When I came out here, I knew I had found cattle country that made Texas look like a desert. And when I started buying up land, I promised myself that I would never be at the mercy of my neighbors again. I grew strong enough to tell my neighbors to go to hell. Powerful enough to have the law working for me instead of against me. And that's how it is, Mr. McClure."

"So I've learned. But nothing stays the same. Things have a way of changing."

"Speaking of change, Mr. McClure," Dunkirk said, leaning back in his chair, "I'll buy your ranch from you at a fair price."

"It's not for sale."

"Oh? I had the impression you might be interested in selling."

"I think not. You see, I came here with a few promises of my own. One was that I was going to stay here, make my life in the Pine Ridge. Die here."

"I'll pay you twice what you gave for the ranch."

"You don't have enough money to buy my ranch. And I came here to serve notice that if you try to squeeze, I'll fight back. I'm willing to walk away from everything that's happened so far, but if there's any more trouble, you'll wish you'd never heard of Dan McClure."

"I don't like threats, Mr. McClure."

"It wasn't a threat."

The old man lifted his hands and waved them placatingly. His lips parted in a bemused smile as though enjoying some private joke. "Now, don't be so feisty young man. I must say, I admire your spirit and courage, though you do give me cause to question your good sense. In any case I find you quite likable, so I'll just disregard your accusatory remarks for the moment. I suggest we declare a truce. Maybe in time, you'll find I'm not quite the ogre I've been made out to be."

Dunkirk was a wily one. He was more politician than rancher. Dan had to give him grudging credit for his self-control. The old man would be a hell of a poker player.

"I'll settle for a truce," Dan said. "A permanent one, I hope. There's no reason we can't get along. Be assured, I'm not going to cut off anybody's water supply."

Chapter 12

SOLOMON PYLE SHIFTED on the bench and swatted at the pesky fly that buzzed at his ear. Dan could see that Sol's patience for his sitting had run out.

"Just a few more minutes, Sol," Dan said. "Then we'll quit for the day."

"My butt's as sore as if I'd spent two days in the saddle," the old cowboy grumbled.

Dan touched his fine brush to the palette, trying to mix the colors into the right pigment of green. His brush swept to the face on the canvas, and he rendered several quick, short strokes to one eye. Close, but not quite right. If he could just persuade the old codger to sit another hour. But it would be hopeless to try to persuade him. It was almost noon and Saturday. Sol would stay long enough to eat, but then he would be in a toot to get home.

After a hurried check on Megan and the hands, Sol would take his weekly bath, shave, and head for Hannah Baker's place. Megan would see him again when it was time for Sunday dinner. It was hard to picture Sol Pyle in the role of an antiquated lothario, but it was a good bet that he was riding five miles to the widow Baker's for more than the roast beef supper and apple pie she fed him every Saturday night. Dan halfway envied the crusty rancher.

He put down his brush, perused the canvas, and nodded approvingly. He was prone to criticizing his own work mercilessly. But this one was coming along quite satisfactorily, he thought, and it had prospects of being quite good if he could just capture the eyes. He took the canvas inside the house, and as he emerged to gather his equipment, he said to Sol, who still sat stiffly on the bench at the edge of the porch, "Hey, it's over, friend. You're free."

"Yeah?"

"I thought you were tired of sitting," Dan said as he retrieved the easel and supplies and stepped back on the porch.

"I'd like to talk a mite, if you got the time."

"Got the time? Hell, yes, I've got the time. You've given me enough of yours the last month. Two or three mornings a week. You'll be losing your job."

"I owed you this . . . for Meggie."

"You didn't owe me anything," Dan said as he went through the door. He called back, "Stay there, Sol. I'll bring you a cup of coffee. Then we'll talk." Something was obviously troubling the old man. He had been quiet and pensive the entire morning.

Dan put the pot of coffee on the coals in the fireplace, and then he cleaned his palette and brushes. He hated the cleanup part; he always would. He dulled the agony by concentrating on a cow grazing sketch he expected to work on in the afternoon. Finally, the unpleasant chore behind him, he poured the steaming coffee into two tin cups and joined Sol on the bench. The older man seemed lost in his thoughts and appeared not to notice Dan's presence until he sat down and handed him the cup.

"I should be finished in another week, Sol," Dan said. "Can you hold out that long?"

The old man looked up and accepted the cup. "What's that?" he said.

"I thought maybe you were getting tired of sitting for the portrait. I said I should be finished in another week."

"Oh, yeah. Can't be soon enough for me. No offense meant."

"That's all right, I understand." Dan hesitated. "You said you wanted to talk about something."

Sol took a deep breath and sighed and sipped at the coffee before he replied. "I want to talk about Meggie a little."

"How is she doing? Has she changed her mind about me?"

"She gets along. Young Nate Coates sticks close like an old cow dog. He won't let no harm come to her. But she's independent as hell and don't like having to be looked after worth a damn. But you can drop by one of these days. I think she'll talk with you some."

"I'm sorry she blames me for what happened."

"Oh, hell, she don't blame nobody. She just don't want you to see her like this. It's got to do with her pride. She's a prideful young lady . . . if you hadn't noticed," he added with a wry smile.

"Is there any improvement at all? Any sign that she's coming out of it?"

"Nope. Like the sawbones up at Fort Robinson said, I guess all we can do is hope. She might never see again, or she might snap out of it all at once. It's been better than a month now . . . don't seem like we can be too hopeful. But you never know. Some things just ain't understood so easy."

Sol gazed out onto the ranch yard, mesmerized by something there that no one else could see.

"The Haskells was burned out last night," he said. "They shotgunned Jubal. Blowed his brains to shit."

Dan tensed and a sinking feeling clutched his belly. "Haskell. I don't think I know the place."

"They got a little spread north of here. Jubal was worthless as tits on a boar hog. Never done nobody no harm . . . outside of slapping his brand on a neighbor's stock when he got the chance. Never stole enough to notice. His missus has dropped six young 'uns, but she's still as pretty as a little red heifer in a flower bed. Reckon she'll sell out to Dunkirk now and look for another man."

"Dunkirk was after the place?"

"Dunkirk's after every place. And my guess is he's about done waitin'. These hills are likely to be soaked with blood before summer's out."

"What makes you say that?"

"You met the old bastard, didn't you? Dunkirk?"

"Yeah," Dan replied.

"Does he look like a man with a lot of years in front him? I ain't seen him for three or four years, but he's no spring chicken."

"No, he's not a young man, and I'd have to say he looked a long ways from the prime of his life."

"Let me tell you something, Dan. The month before he had Ben Grant killed off—"

"You don't know that Dunkirk was responsible," Dan interrupted.

The old man ignored him. "As I was saying, a month before he had Ben killed, he and Ben had a big set to over at the Diamond D. They always fought like a pair of bobcats in a sack. They went clear back to Texas days, you know."

"That's what Dunkirk told me."

"Anyhow, old Woody, he told Ben that his string was running out and come hell or high water, he aimed to have the Diamond D all put together before he croaked. Meaning he was going to gobble up the small ranches hereabouts before he rode off to hell. Nope, you mark my words . . . Haskells' won't be the last. Not by a long shot."

"You said you wanted to talk about Megan. What does all this have to do with her?"

Sol did not look at him, his opaque eyes still fixed on the invisible spot in the yard. "I went to see a law wrangler yesterday, a lawyer in Medicine Hill by the name of Lucas Battie. He's kind of a contrary old fart, but he's honest as the day is long. I had my will made out. It's in Battie's safe; I wanted you to know that. If I said anything to Meggie about it, she'd get herself worked up."

"I see." Sol's conversation made Dan uncomfortable, but he could see the old man needed to get things off his chest. He was talking like a man who did not expect to live long. A man who had been struck with some premonition of death. Dan had encountered other such men in the Army, and what bothered him now was the accuracy with which they had predicted their fate. Or had they simply been victims of self-fulfilling prophecies?

"I don't think I ever mentioned it," Sol said, "but the Bar G's always been handled as one spread and Ben Grant owned a big part of it. But I got three sections in my own name. One of them snuggles up against your place. Of course, Dunkirk knows all this. Anyhow, I had me some money of my own when we moved up from Texas, and I decided to buy up some land on my own. Ben didn't have the money to buy all he needed anyhow, so I just leased him what I had to go with his own. Sometimes he paid cash rent; sometimes he paid in cows; sometimes he couldn't pay at all. It didn't matter none. Ben and Meggie, well, they was family." He turned his head toward Dan now, his eyes meeting Dan's evenly. "Son, I'd like to think we've become friends of a sort."

"We have," Dan said.

"It would give me a lot of peace if you would promise me something."

"Name it."

"Well, first off, when I cash in my chips one of these days, I'd like you to take Meggie in to see Lawyer Battie. Then I want you to see that my will's carried out to the letter."

"You'll probably outlive me, but when the times comes, if I'm around I'll do it. You can count on it."

"And will you sort of keep an eye on the Bar G? Help out Meggie when you can. She'd scream like hell if she knew I'd asked you this, but if she don't get her sight back, she's going to need extra help for a spell. I'd rest a lot better knowing she'd have it."

"She'll have it, whether she likes it or not. But Sol, I don't understand why you're talking like this."

"No reason in particular. A man just never knows what's over the ridge," Sol replied unconvincingly, "and I just want to be sure Meggie's looked after. She's unpredictable as hell. More so since the night Ben got killed."

"What do you mean?"

"Well, Meggie always halfway blamed herself for Ben's getting killed. You see, her and old Ben had a squabble that night. A young drifter who'd been riding roundup over at the Rocking R was sparkin' Meggie that spring. He wasn't a bad kid, but he didn't have enough sense to spit downwind. Ben didn't think the kid was good enough for Meggie. I didn't either, for that matter. But Meggie didn't see it that way. I guess it was past time for her to lose her heart to some cowpoke. Anyhow, after her and Ben locked horns, she tore out of the house and rode off like a bat out of hell. When she didn't come back, me and some of the hands rode out to find her. While we was gone, somebody turned a shotgun loose on Ben. Meggie got home before we did. She's the one who found Ben on the porch."

"It must have been terrible for her," Dan said.

"Yep. But you know, I never saw that gal drop a tear. I s'pose she did, but not while I was around. She growed up real fast after that; finally saw the drifter for what he was. But she's been skittish as a colt since that night. That's why I'm asking you to stand by her. She'll need a friend at her side."

"If the time comes, she'll have one."

Sol seemed satisfied at that and turned away, but Dan had a feeling there was still something unsaid, and he had a hunch he knew what it was.

"There are some things a man carries alone when he rides through life," Sol said, his voice melancholy, "things that are best carried alone. But when you get close to the end of the trail, you get to thinkin'. Pretty soon, you ain't going to be nothing but so much worm food and nobody's going to know about this load you took on . . . unless you tell somebody."

"Is there something else you'd like to tell me, Sol?"

"I don't know. There's something I'd like for somebody to know, but I don't rightly know why. Maybe I just think somebody ought to know about it, in case it might help out someday. I wouldn't want Meggie to ever find out unless it just had to be for some good reason. I don't know. Maybe I just need to fess up, but it's been gnawing at my innards lately."

"Are you wanting to tell me that Megan Grant is your daughter?" Dan asked softly.

The old rancher jerked upright. He turned to Dan, his eyes incredulous, his mouth gaping open. "Jesus Christ, Dan, don't sneak up on a fellar like that. How in the hell did you know?"

"The eyes. Nothing else. Just the eyes. I'm an artist, Sol. There aren't many who would ever notice, but I guessed the night Megan was injured."

"I'll be damned. I'll be double damned. It makes me proud as hell to think somebody saw something of me in Meggie. Still, it scares the piss out of me that somebody else might see it, too."

"Does it really matter so much? Maybe you should tell Megan."

"Oh, God, no. That can't never be. As far as Meggie's concerned, Ben Grant was her daddy, and he for damn sure was in the ways that count. She might have growed from my seed, but he fed her and taught her and raised her up. He was an educated man with breeding. He gave her things I never could have. Meggie loved Ben as her daddy. It wouldn't be right to take that away."

"I doubt if it would," Dan said.

"Maybe not. But I'd still shame Meggie's mother . . . God rest her soul." Sol's eyes clouded and traces of moisture gathered at the corners of his eyes. "Meggie's like her spittin' image, you know. Except for the eyes. Rita's was dark, like two pieces of shiny coal. She was Mexican, daughter of one of the dons that lived in one of them big haciendas. The old man never forgave her after she run off with Ben Grant. Ben worked for old Dunkirk in them days, but he wasn't cut out for riding for somebody else, not for long. He had some book learnin' from someplace and was good with figures. If the war hadn't come along, he'd been a rich man by now. He wasn't fifty yet when he was killed. He would have been a big man in the county, too, in time. Dunkirk knew that. The difference between him and Dunkirk, though, was that Ben had principles that he'd believe in and fight for. That's why him and Dunkirk had a falling out."

"Dunkirk told me about it," Dan said. "According to him, he got burned out in Texas . . . lost his wife there."

"Ben didn't have nothin' to do with the things that happened at Dunkirk's ranch. Hell, he was too busy gettin' ready for war to fool with that nonsense. And Ben wasn't the kind of man that fought his neighbors. The war, that was the problem. Ben joined up. The Johnny Rebs made him a captain. The damn fool took off for four years. Meggie was born almost ten months after Ben rode out, and Rita birthed before her time. The jackass left me behind to look after things. I didn't give a damn about the war, but I was fifteen years older than Ben, so I suppose he figured Rita was safe. He guessed wrong. A woman gets lonely with her man gone. She just can't help it. And I was there. I loved that woman. God, how I loved that woman. So dark and pretty. Soft spoken and gentle. She always had a smile. No matter how much she hurt, she always had a smile. It just happened. That's all I can say. Wasn't nobody's fault. It just happened. She loved me, I know that, but nothing would have ever happened if her man had stayed home. She loved Ben. She always did. Does that make sense?"

"Yes, I can understand it."

"She wasn't no slut," Sol hastened. "She was just too damn loving. Too hot blooded. Maybe it was her Mexican blood. And me, it was my misfortune that the good Lord got mixed up and put my brains between my legs."

"You've been too hard on yourself, Sol. Like you said, it just happened. Life's that way. You just have to accept it and go on. Would you rather there had never been a Megan Grant?"

The old man's eyes narrowed as he looked at Dan questioningly. "Dear God, no. I never thought of it that way. Meggie's what made my life worth living. I ain't much on religion, but as far as I'm concerned, Meggie's my life after death."

"And Ben Grant, Meggie must have been something special to him, too."

"Damn right, she was. Meggie was everything to Ben. Hell, when he come home from the war you should have seen his face when he saw little Meggie. He lit up like a goddamn candle. Ben moved back in the bedroom with Rita and never asked no questions. But I've wondered a lot of times. You know, they was married nigh on five years before Rita got with child, and Ben and Rita shared a bed for five years after the war and there wasn't no more young 'uns. Do you think Ben knew about me and Rita and Meggie?"

"I can't say. But if he did, he must have understood. Isn't that all that matters?"

"Damn it, son, you sure got a way of puttin' things that makes a man feel right."

"Sometimes it just takes somebody else to sort out what you already know deep down," Dan said. He stood up and stretched his long legs. "Now, why don't you just sit here a bit longer, and I'll rustle up some grub."

Sol beamed up at Dan. "Don't spare yourself on my account. Damned if I couldn't eat a side of beef right now."

Chapter 13

SOLOMON PYLE HAD barely ridden out of sight, and Dan had just started to get out his oils for another session at the canvas when he heard the whinny of a horse in the yard. Instinctively, he snatched up his gun belt which hung on a nail near the door. He buckled it on and checked the chambers of the revolver before he pulled the curtain back slightly and peered out the window. It was Elizabeth Dunkirk astride a thickly muscled black stallion. He opened the door and walked out onto the porch.

"I said I was going to stop by for a visit," Liz Dunkirk said, her full lips parted in a mischievous smile.

Dan stepped off the porch and looked up at her. Her golden hair was tied back with a royal blue ribbon and glistened in the afternoon sun; her laughing eyes were translucent lakes of sapphire. The tailored riding outfit that clung to her shapely frame seemed more appropriate to Eastern society. She was nothing less than stunning in it.

"I was led to believe that I would be honored with a private showing of your paintings. Am I invited in, or would you prefer that I ride on?"

"Of course you're invited in. You'll have to pardon me, I'm just not accustomed to such charming guests." He moved to assist her down from the stallion, but she swept off the horse easily and had dismounted before he reached her. He took the horse's reins. "Let me put up your horse," he said, observing that the stallion's neck and flanks were moist and sticky with sweat and that he was frothing somewhat at the mouth. He had been ridden hard, unnecessarily hard, for a casual jaunt. "He's about done in," Dan said. "I'll take him into the barn and rub him down. He'd better go slow on the water or he'll founder. If you like, you can go on into the house and look at the paintings while I see to the horse. Help yourself to a cup of coffee, if you don't mind it strong and bitter."

"Thank you. I'll do just that."

Dan's eyes followed her as she glided toward the house with a slight, but enticing, sway of the hips. *Damn, Elizabeth Dunkirk.* She knew he was watching. It was a good bet she knew what she was doing to him. He was vulnerable as hell right now; he would have to be wary of this witch, or she would cast a spell on him that would make him beg to sell his soul to the devil.

Dan put up the stallion in the barn and watered and grained the horse. By the time he left the barn, Elizabeth Dunkirk had emerged from the house and was sailing across the ranch yard to meet him.

"You made a quick tour," he said. "Do you want to go back in and get the free lecture that goes with it?"

"Oh, it's too nice to be cooped up inside," she said. "Let's walk into the hills. Daddy says your place is the Garden of Eden of the Pine Ridge. I'd like to see for my-self." She linked her arm in his and tugged him toward the ponderosa-cloaked hills that backed the house.

The Garden of Eden. And was Liz Dunkirk Eve incar-nate? If so, he was damned if he wouldn't mind being Adam right now. He had hoped to show her his paintings, though, and was rather disappointed that she had not shown more interest in his work. On the other hand, he admitted, he tended to take his work too seriously and to be a little professorial about it. He probably would have bored her to death.

She seemed to guess what he was thinking. "I honest-ly did enjoy your paintings," she said, "but I must confess I don't know a great deal about art. I've been to galleries, but I never found them very exciting. I prefer real things and real people to paintings."

"Sometimes when you paint," Dan said, "you see more of the real people and real things. You see things you didn't realize were there before, and the challenge is to make others see them, too."

"That's a nice thought," she said, "but I'm afraid I wouldn't have the patience to see those things. But I'm intrigued by a man who does and by a man who has the skill and the intellect to paint such things. Yes, you're a very intriguing man, Daniel McClure . . . and you must be a lusty one."

He was taken aback for a moment, uncertain how to reply. "I'm afraid I don't understand."

"Your paintings. The naked ladies and the other women. You must like women."

"Well, of course I like women. But I like to think that someone would see more than an artist's lust when they looked at my paintings."

She was silent as they strolled higher into the hills and finally inched their way to the top of the ridge that rimmed the valley. Dan helped her scale the tooth-like outcropping of rock that offered a natural vantage point from which they could survey most of the ranch.

"Breathtaking," she announced, leaning heavily against him. "Daddy was right. It is the most beautiful place in the whole Pine Ridge." She pointed to the ragged break in the steep hills to the south. "That's where Beaver Creek flows onto the Diamond D, isn't it?"

"Yes."

The creeks were fed by tentacle-like fingers of water that swept along the valley floor and sliced through the lush green grass and meandered their way to the creek bed that snaked its way through the meadow.

"And those are where the springs feed the creek?"

"Yes, that's right," he said.

"For some reason, springs break out all over this part of the valley."

She seemed very knowledgeable about this ranch, genuinely interested. Too knowledgeable? Too interested?

"You can't blame Daddy for wanting this," she said, as they clambered down from the outcropping.

"No, I can't blame him," Dan said, as they began working their way down a deer trail that twisted in the direction of the house. "Not for wanting it. I don't blame him for trying to buy it as long as his methods are legal and ethical."

She was quiet as they continued their descent, until the trail began to widen and finally opened into a tiny grassy clearing that was set nest-like on a little mesa midway between the ridge crest and the ranch buildings below. She stopped abruptly there and whirled on him.

"What did you mean when you said 'legal and ethical'? About Daddy trying to buy your land?" Her eyes were ice blue now, the fine line of her jaw set firm.

Dan could see she was angry, but she had not lost control of her temper. "I shouldn't have said that . . . you're a guest. I didn't intend to accuse."

"But you've heard things about Daddy and the Diamond D, haven't you?"

"I'd be lying if I said no. Yes, people say your father wants a solid patch of Diamond D on the county map. That he's obsessed with swallowing up all the small ranches that break up the Diamond D range. And especially that he plans to get my place and the Bar G . . . at any cost."

"That doesn't mean he'd kill people for it."

"No, and I'm not convinced of that myself. But someone almost killed me, and they tried to kill Megan Grant. Somebody shot Ben Grant, and I've been told others died before I came here. And then last night a man named

Jubal Haskell was murdered, and his ranch burned out. Did you know about that?"

"Yes, I heard about it. Terrible thing. I had a wagon load of food and clothing sent over to Mrs. Haskell and her children. Daddy's very generous with things like that."

"Did your father want the Haskell ranch?"

"Yes, of course. I won't deny that. The Diamond D surrounded it, but that's not evidence that he had anyone killed. Not that Jubal Haskell didn't need killing. He was a damned cow thief. Daddy put up with it because he felt sorry for Jubal's kids."

"I see."

"But you don't believe."

"It's not that. I just don't know, but I hope to find out soon. People usually don't kill without a reason, and your father's the only one who seems to have a reason . . . even though it's not a valid one."

"Daddy couldn't. He doesn't even leave the house."

"He doesn't? Why not?"

"Hardly anyone knows. He can't walk. He's paralyzed from his waist down. His horse threw him a few years back. When you went to see my father, he remained seated behind the desk, didn't he?"

"Yes."

"That's the only place he'll see people . . . in his study, behind the desk. That's why he doesn't like unnecessary visitors. He doesn't want them to know. He's afraid they'll think he's weak and take advantage of him."

"I can't imagine anyone taking advantage of your father," Dan said.

"Clay Sutherly does."

"That's a strange thing to say about your betrothed."

"I'm not engaged to marry Clay Sutherly. If I wanted to marry Clay, we'd have been married a long time ago. Daddy's been pressing me for better than a year. The marriage is in Daddy's and Clay's heads. Daddy picked Clay out for me six or seven years ago while I was still attending school in the East. He thought Clay was smart enough and strong enough to hold the ranch and to build on what Daddy left me. You see, I'm just a woman." She spat it out sarcastically.

"I don't understand."

"I think you do. Daddy loves me. He'd give me anything. But he should have had a son. Daughters can't take over a ranch and run a cattle empire. That's what Daddy and men like him think anyway. I know the Diamond D forwards and backwards, and I've had to dig it out on my own. I've got business sense. I'm every bit as shrewd and hard-headed as my father, but he can't see it. I've tried to broach the subject, but he just chuckles and tells me to buy a new bonnet or a new gown, just like he'd offer a child a piece of hard rock candy."

"I think your father underestimates his daughter," Dan said.

She clasped her hands behind her back and turned away and began pacing in front of Dan. "Damn right, he does. And if Clay Sutherly wasn't around, I could convince Daddy. I know I could. What I said before, it's true: Clay does take advantage of Daddy. Clay runs the ranch. He takes his orders from Daddy, but then does what he damn well pleases. He thinks the ranch is already his, but he's worried. Daddy's failed a lot this past year, and Clay wants to get married . . . bad. Daddy's made arrangements for Clay to manage the ranch when he dies, but Clay gets a share of the ranch only if we're married. Daddy's angry at me. He wants us to get married, too, before the summer's out. I told him I would die first, that he just wanted me to be a broodmare for the grandchildren Clay would sire. I told Daddy I'd geld the bastard if he tried to touch me."

Dan smiled in spite of himself. She would do it, too. Damned, if she wouldn't.

"That's how Clay sees me, too . . . as a broodmare. Ready to mount when he needs it. Somebody to drop a foal once a year." She stopped mid-stride and whirled toward Dan. "If somebody at the Diamond D's burning out ranches, having people murdered, it's not Woodson Dunkirk. It's Clay Sutherly. You can bet your ass on it."

"I'd like to hear more about Sutherly," Dan said.

She stared back at Dan silently, the ice in her eyes melting now, giving way to warm, still pools. *God, she was beautiful*. She was an enchantress. They could never be friends. He doubted if he could truly like her, much less love her. Still, grudgingly, he admired her spirit and her strength and was fascinated by her brashness. Above all, he wanted her.

Slowly, Liz Dunkirk's slender fingers moved to the top button of her shirt and unfastened it, displaying the provocative cleavage between ample white breasts. "I asked if you were a lusty man," she said. "You never answered."

Dan stepped toward Liz Dunkirk and collected her in his arms, covered her lips with his, savoring the yielding softness of the body that pressed tight against him. Her fingernails dug into his shoulders, and she clung to him with eagerness leaving no doubt in his mind that her body was attuned to his, succumbing with his to the raging desires that tore mercilessly through them. She pulled him down into the bed of grass, and he became

Adam, giving and taking, surrendering himself to the wiles of Eve in this Garden of Eden.

Chapter 14

I
T WAS LATE afternoon, and the fiery orange sun was sliced in half by the west ridge when they strolled hand in hand from the ponderosa and came out onto the ranch yard. They had almost reached the house before Dan saw the blond-bearded man who was staring at them from where he stood between a buckskin gelding and Liz Dunkirk's black stallion. Reflexively, Dan released Liz Dunkirk's hand and his own edged closer to his revolver.

When Elizabeth Dunkirk caught sight of Sutherly, she smiled with feigned delight and waved at the Diamond D foreman. "Why, Clay," she said, "fancy meeting you here. Did you come to see Mr. McClure's paintings, too?"

"If I did, I don't think I'd find them up on the ridge," said Sutherly, his voice surly, his eyes boring in on Dan.

"Mr. McClure was just showing me his ranch. There's a beautiful view from the ridge."

"I'll bet."

"Now, Clay, don't be pouty."

Crimson spread over Sutherly's face. "It's late. I've saddled your horse. Your old man will be worried sick."

She stopped not far from the horses. Dan could see that she had been compelled to rein in her temper and that now she was choosing her words carefully. "The old man's name is Mr. Dunkirk," she said, "and you would do well to remember that. And I assure you that Mr. Dunkirk will not be worried. He will take his supper alone and fall asleep shortly thereafter. In the morning, he will have no idea when we arrived home. And one further thing, Clay Sutherly, I do not need an escort in this county. I know the Pine Ridge, and I am perfectly capable of taking care of myself."

"Don't be so sure. These are violent times."

"Horse shit," she snapped. She turned to Dan, and to his surprise, reached up and pulled his head to her. She kissed him lightly on the cheek and whispered in his ear, "Kill him for me, Dan, please. Soon." She stepped back and smiled, "Thank you, Dan, for a lovely afternoon. I enjoyed your paintings. I see so much of you in them." She turned away and scurried to her horse.

Dan looked up and met Sutherly's glare. There was death written in those eyes. Like it or not, he might have to kill Sutherly. Especially if Elizabeth Dunkirk had her way. She was using him like a pawn on a chessboard. He had no doubt about it.

As Sutherly and Liz Dunkirk galloped away, Dan wondered when he would see her again. His heart raced at the thought of it. Soon, he hoped.

Chapter 15

A COOL MORNING BREEZE caressed Megan's face as she cantered the pinto across the meadow that fringed the Bar G corral and catch pens. A sage hen cackled, and Megan heard the frantic fluttering of its wings off to her right as it escaped the gelding's hooves. She no doubt had a nest close by, and Megan formed an image of the plump hen in her mind, her multi-hues of brown camouflaging her now as the torrid July sun started to bake the grass dry and cook away the green. No one had told her this. She knew it from the crisp rustling that the grass made against the horse's legs as they swept through the meadow.

The sun would be scorching later, but now it was a morning made for a ride. It was Sunday-morning peaceful. The nearest church was a good ten miles away, but somehow the horses and cattle and all of God's creatures seemed to know Sunday morning was a time for quiet. She toyed with the notion of letting her pinto carry her into the hills but thought better of it. Nate would get a burr under his tail and head after her the minute he saw her riding away, and she wanted to be alone now. She liked Nate's company and was very fond of him. In time, she might even marry him, like he had asked her to. She remembered him as slender and wiry, and boyishly handsome, decidedly more attractive than Dan McClure, she reminded herself. Why did she always compare every man to Dan McClure?

She reined the pinto to the right, wheeled him around, and reversed her course, taking quiet satisfaction in the smoothness of the maneuver. Yes, she would travel the ridge on horseback again, drink it in with her remaining senses. Touch, smell, hear the things she could not see. She had a life to live, and she would not spend it groping her way within the confines of the ranch house.

As she nudged the gelding across the meadow, she heard the thudding of a horse's hooves angling toward her from the left and to the rear. It was Nate's mare. She could tell by the horse's rhythmic gait and the softness of its step. Megan slowed the gelding and then reined it to a halt as Nate Coates pulled even with her.

"What is it, Nate?" she asked, trying to conceal the irritation in her voice.

He hesitated. "You got a visitor."

"I'm in no mood for playing games, Nate. Who is it?"

"Well, it's that artist, the big fellow that took over Ike Hanson's spread."

"Didn't you tell him I was busy?"

"Yep, I sure did. But he ain't takin' no. He's waitin' over by the corral. Said I could call you in, or he'd ride out himself."

"Tell him to go to hell," she snapped.

"I don't think he's going to leave."

"Oh, all right. Tell him I'll be back in a minute. I want to take another swing past the windmill." Without waiting for a reply, she dug her heels gently into the pinto's flanks, and he lurched forward and raced away at full gallop. As she streaked across the prairie land, her sable tresses flying in the wind, Megan scolded herself for her curtness with Nate. He was so devoted to her, like a faithful collie: loyal and unquestioning and obedient. But she was so tired of being nursed and coddled like an orphan calf. If Sol and Nate had their ways, she would spend the rest of her life in a rocking chair with the two of them waiting on her hand and foot, slobbering over her like a couple of mama cows over a newborn.

Her thoughts turned to Dan McClure. Why was he here? She had not talked to him since the morning she learned of her blindness, better than three months now. He had ridden over frequently after her injury, but she had steadfastly refused to see him. Finally, he had given up. But Sol conversed with him regularly, almost daily, over at Dan's place up until a few weeks earlier when he had stopped "sittin' for a picture," as he called it. Sol had told her that Dan thought she blamed him for her blindness. How could he be so stupid? He had saved her life, although for a time she had not been certain she was grateful for it.

No, it was something else, but she could not quite put her finger on it. For some reason, she did not want Dan to see her when she was less than strong and totally independent. And, in a way, she was frightened of any friendship with Dan McClure. He was a complex man, a challenging man. But how could she understand him, learn all she wanted to learn about him if she could not see his paintings? For the key to Dan McClure was in his work and what he painted and how he painted.

She heard the squeaking of the windmill and the sudden rush of water splashing into a tank off to her right. She brushed her right rein against the pinto's neck; the gelding angled to the right, and they swept around the wooden tower and headed across the pasture toward the corrals. Megan gave the pony free rein, knowing he would carry her home.

Soon, Megan could hear the whinnying and stomping of horses that told her they were nearing the corral. She slowed the pinto gradually into a walk.

"Just whoa up, Meg," came Nate's voice from off to the right. "I'll take your horse and help you down."

"No." Her tone said it was a command. Megan could hear the blowing and nickering of other horses that were, no doubt, pressing their muzzles between the planks of the corral fence as they greeted the pinto, and she knew she was next to the corral when the pinto stopped on its own accord. She dismounted and, groping for the corral fence, tied the gelding there.

"You handled him real good this morning, Meg, real good," Nate said.

"Why shouldn't I have?" she asked curtly.

"Mr. McClure's about ten paces behind you next to the corral. Do you want me to help you over?"

"No, but thank you," she said, again regretting her sharpness with the cowboy. "But you can put Pirate up, if you like. I won't be riding anymore this morning."

"Sure, Meg."

Nate Coates unhitched the pinto and led it away as Megan, brushing her fingertips lightly along the fence boards for bearing, walked slowly towards Dan.

"Good morning, Megan," Dan said when she was within four or five feet. "It's been a long time. Too long."

Megan halted, grateful for the discrete signal he had given her. "Yes, it has been a long time."

"I thought I'd drop by and chew the fat with Sol awhile. Nate says he's gone, but he seemed a little mysterious about it."

"He's, uh, visiting Mrs. Baker. He should be home by dinner time. He always is."

From the sound of Dan's voice, Megan guessed that he was not facing her, but rather looking out onto the pasture, probably leaning against the corral fence. She turned and rested her own back against the fence, folding her arms across her chest, fixing her sightless eyes toward the meadow.

"I wish he'd stick closer to home these days," she said. "Ever since Jubal Haskell was killed, I've worried when Sol's gone too long."

"But you know where he's at now. Are you sure it's not Mrs. Baker that's worrying you?"

"Why do you say that?"

"Sol thinks you don't care much for Mrs. Baker. I get the same feeling."

"It's not Mrs. Baker. She's a very likable person. It's what she is."

"I don't understand."

"I forgot, you're new around here. Let me put it this way: Mrs. Baker has other gentlemen callers. One for every night of the week, I'm told. Several of them are married men."

Dan laughed. "You're concerned for Sol's virtue? I'd think he would be old enough to handle that part of his life by himself."

"Oh, I know, and he's been seeing the widow Baker for years. But when I was growing up, I always thought of Sol as sort of a god. Daddy always said that Sol couldn't do wrong in my eyes. I guess he was right." She smiled in spite of herself. "Oh, what a shock it was to me when I figured out why Sol was visiting Hannah Baker every Saturday night. For a spell, I was a woman scorned. I was sixteen at the time . . . couldn't look Sol in the eye for weeks after. I hardly spoke to him. But he won me back. He always did."

"Don't judge him too harshly. Be glad for whatever warmth and comfort he receives from Mrs. Baker. Sol's led a very unselfish life; indulge him in this. And think kindly of Mrs. Baker, too. I sometimes wonder if the Hannah Bakers of this world aren't doing more to relieve human misery than a dozen pious preachers."

Megan thought of the seductive, nude Angela in Dan's painting. "Of course, I'd expect you to understand people like that better than most."

"Maybe," Dan said, "but I wasn't talking about prostitutes specifically. I was talking about people in general. It's damn hard to crawl under somebody else's skin and know what personal hells they've suffered, or understand why people do what they do sometimes. Over the years, I've decided that maybe it's best to let people do what they want as long as they don't hurt anyone else in the process. You know, I think that's what this country's all about but we tend to forget it sometimes."

Deep down, she agreed, but was in no mood to concede it. "You have a lecture for every subject don't you?" She could hear him shift the weight of his feet.

"Yes, that's a failing of mine."

He was facing her now, but she did not turn toward him.

"My work necessarily forces me into a somewhat solitary existence, and when I have someone to talk to, I suppose I try to make up for lost time. And for some reason,

I seem to run off at the mouth when I'm with you. I'm sorry."

"I don't mind. I truly don't. I'm just witchy today." He apparently wasn't going to disagree with her.

"You were a little tough on Nate," Dan said. "You shouldn't be. He adores you, you know. For that matter, I'd say he's in love with you."

"I know."

"Marriage?"

"Maybe. I can't say, not now."

"He seems to be a nice young man. Handsome as the devil. Gentle and considerate. He's intensely loyal to you. He'd be a faithful husband and an easy man to live with."

"Yes, I think he would," Megan said.

"But he's not right for you. You'd make each other miserable. Do you know that?"

"I didn't ask your opinion."

"No, I guess you didn't. Well, I suppose I'd better be on my way. I'll catch Sol some other time."

He did not move, and she could feel him staring at her. Damn him. Why did he have to show up just when things were beginning to fall into place? "You can stay for dinner if you'd like," she said grudgingly. "Sol will be disappointed if he misses you."

"It wouldn't be any trouble?"

"No, it wouldn't be any trouble. There's plenty for another mouth."

"I'll stay."

"Meg? Mr. McClure?"

It was Nate's voice, and Megan sensed an urgency in it. She turned toward the voice and heard the crunch of his boots in the crusty earth, as he dashed toward her. "What is it, Nate?" she asked, her heart pounding like a hammer in her breast.

"It's Hannah Baker's place. Charlie was rounding up some strays over on the east ridge when he saw it."

"Saw what?" Megan asked.

"Smoke. Lots of it. Too much for a chimney," he said. "Charlie knew Sol was over there, so he high-tailed it back here to get some help."

"Oh, dear God," Megan gasped. She felt her body growing numb and was only vaguely aware that Dan had moved to her side and had wrapped his arm firmly around her shoulders, steadying her there while she sorted out her thoughts.

"Nate," Dan ordered, "round up any hands you can find. Tell them to saddle up and be ready to ride."

"Ain't more than two or three on the place, Mr. McClure, it being Sunday and all."

"Well, find them."

"Yes, sir." The cowboy wheeled and headed across the yard for the bunkhouse.

"And Nate," Dan called after him.

The cowboy stopped in his tracks and turned, "Yes, sir?"

"You stay with Megan. Saddle a couple of horses and be ready to ride just in case there's trouble. Don't be a goddamned hero, do you understand?"

Megan, fighting off the shock that had almost overpowered her, stepped free from Dan's arm. "I'm going, too."

"No, you aren't."

"Who do you think you are? You talk like a damned general or something. It's my ranch. They're my hands. I'll go if I damn well please."

His strong hands grabbed her shoulders, gripping them like twin vices, his face nearly touching hers. "Think, Megan. Put your damned pride aside for a minute. Can you keep up with us? Do you want to slow us down? What if there's shooting? Will you help Sol by being there?"

A spasm ripped through her belly as she shook convulsively for a moment; her eyes began to burn and tears started to stream down her cheeks. "I'll stay," she said. "Now, get going. I can find my way back to the house. I can do that much." She felt his lips brush across her forehead before he released his grip and hurried away.

Chapter 16

WHEN DAN AND the three Bar G riders rode into the flatland a mile down the valley from Hannah Baker's farm, he knew instantly the need to hurry was past. Thick, black smoke that curled skyward told him the burning was in its last stages, and all that they would find there would be the smoldering charred remains of the farm buildings.

They were downwind, and his army duty in the Sioux wars had taught him the smell of burning flesh, and the stench that seared his nostrils now was decidedly that. He could only hope it was not human.

It was likely the attackers had departed hours ago, but Dan ordered the riders to spread out as they cautiously approached the smoking rubble that had been a house and barn and other outbuildings. Dan slipped his Winchester from the saddle holster, cradling it across his horse's neck as they rode in. He signaled the others to hold up as he dismounted and walked slowly into the farmyard. He caught sight of Sol's twisted body in front of the house; he spied the woman's off to the side. They had not been spared, either. In fact, as near as he could see, the marauders had not overlooked a single living thing in their slaughter.

He waved in the riders, went over to Sol's body, and knelt down. He saw that the old man's rifle was not far away, so he knew Sol had put up a fight before they smoked him out. The corpse lay face up, but Dan saw no one he recognized there. He had learned to steel himself from death as much as a man could; he did not flinch at the empty staring eyes or the bloody, bullet-shredded chest and throat. He grieved for what was gone, not for the soulless, bloated corpse sprawled in the dust.

He got up and walked over to the woman's body. She had been a buxom woman, younger than he would have guessed, probably no more than forty-five. The chestnut hair that framed her face, dirty and matted now, would have been pretty the night before. He could not tell much about her face. She had been bludgeoned to death, probably with a rifle butt, and the contorted broken face and skull gave no clue to her earlier appearance.

"Bastards," he whispered. "Murdering bastards."

He turned when he heard the muffled clip-clop of hooves behind him and looked up to see three sober-faced cowboys. Charlie Gates, an old hand, shook his head sadly. The other two, like Nate Coates, not much more than boys, stared wide-eyed at the macabre scene. The two sat there, frozen in their saddles, their faces ashen. One, likely both, would chuck up breakfast before their work was finished this morning.

Charlie Gates dismounted and hobbled over to Dan, one hand resting on a gimpy leg. "I came up from Texas with Sol Pyle and Ben Grant. Now they've both saddled a cloud, and I'm the only one left. They shouldn't have died like this, neither one. Not in these times."

"Not in any time," Dan said, his eyes scanning the rubble and carnage of the barnyard, trying to ferret out an answer, a clue to what happened there and why. And who.

"What's going to happen to the little lady?" the stumpy cowhand asked. "First her daddy, then being struck blind, now poor old Sol. Dear God, what's she going to do now?"

"She'll go on," Dan said softly.

"Who's going to break the news to her?" Charlie asked.

"I will. She'll be waiting. I'll head back to the Bar G after I take a good look around here. If you can round up something to dig a grave with, bury the woman. But bring Sol back to the ranch. I don't think you can scare up an extra horse; you'll probably have to lash together a travois."

Dan paced the barnyard while the cowhands reluctantly started their gut-wrenching chores. From the tracks in the yard, he surmised there had been a half-dozen or more men. They had probably struck about dawn. Hannah Baker was in her nightdress, and Sol was shirtless and barefooted. He'd probably just had time to pull on his trousers after he heard some commotion outside. Dan paused when he spotted splotches of discolored dust some fifty feet in front of the house. He knelt down and touched a finger to the earth. It was sticky and caking, but there was no doubt about it: blood. A lot of it. They had not taken Sol without a fight, and he had done some damage of his own before he surrendered. If he could find out who took a bullet this morning, it would unlock the door to a lot of answers. He had little doubt that the Diamond D, or someone there, was behind the killings and the terrorizing, but he did not want to execute a counter attack without proof. One thing was for certain: he could not paint again while this trouble brewed in the hills. Like it or not, it was time to put down the brush and pick up the gun.

"Charlie," Dan called as he headed for his horse. Charlie Gates put down the charred stub of a board that he was struggling to hollow out a shallow grave with and got up and limped over to Dan. "I'm heading back to the Bar G to tell Megan."

"You ain't got my envy for that job," Charlie said.

"Charlie, how many small ranchers do you suppose there are in this valley? How many are bounded by the Diamond D?"

The older man rubbed the stubble on his chin with a calloused hand. "Damn, it's hard to say, Mr. McClure. Maybe twenty or twenty-five, all told. The majority are one and two man operations. The Bar G is the biggest of the small ones. We have six hands year-round and hire extras in spring and fall. There's maybe a half dozen three and four-hand ranches. Of course, that don't tell the story 'cause I ain't counting kids for hands, and there's a passel of big families in this valley. Fertile for cattle and kids, Ben Grant always used to say."

"Charlie, would you be able to pick out a half dozen ranchers who could be trusted? More specifically, ones who could be trusted not to carry tales to Woodson Dunkirk or the Diamond D? I need men with influence, but closed-mouthed men, for now. And men with some iron in their bellies. I don't know these people; I'll have to depend on you. Could you find them?"

"Easier than I can brand a sucking calf. It shouldn't be no chore. Lots of folks in these parts is scared, but there's some that maybe ain't scared enough. Just tell me what you want."

"Tomorrow, I want you to ride out and talk to those men, tell them about what happened to Sol and Mrs. Baker. Then tell them that Megan Grant would like to have them drop over for dinner Wednesday noon. Just say she needs their help. Don't mention my name."

"This is a busy time of year for daytime socializing, Mr. McClure," Charlie said.

"Well, I don't want to take these men away from their homes at night; they shouldn't leave their families alone. I think they'll come during the day, though. From what I've seen and heard, there's not much most of these Pine Ridge people won't do to help a neighbor."

Charlie kicked aimlessly at a clump of dirt. "Mr. McClure, there's one thing I've been wonderin' about."

"What's that, Charlie?"

"The sheriff. I don't suppose it would do much good, but shouldn't somebody ride in and tell him?"

"I intend to do that, Charlie. But not till tomorrow or the next day. I doubt if he'll even bother to ride out, so there's no hurry. Mr. Keaton seems to know his county; he may already know more about this than we do."

The cowboy wrinkled his brow, squinted one eye, and looked at Dan quizzically.

Chapter 17

THE LAWYER'S OFFICE was drab and austere. From an artist's viewpoint, the color scheme and simple furnishings would be categorized as ugly brown. Lucas Battie, a rotund, bald man with a cherubic face peered over wire-rimmed spectacles at his visitors this scorching Tuesday afternoon. The room was humid and suffocating, and the half-open windows might well have been closed so still was the air outside. Battie dabbed at his forehead with a rumpled handkerchief.

"If you like, I'll proceed with the reading," he said in a high-pitched voice. His face was undertaker grim.

Dan glanced at Megan, whose own face was expressionless. Damn, she was a striking young woman, even in mourning black. He had never seen her in a dress before this morning. Somehow, it brought out a sophisticated side of her that working ranch garb tried to obscure.

"Yes, you can go ahead," Dan said.

The lawyer read aloud, "Last will and testament of Solomon George Pyle. I, Solomon George Pyle, being of sound mind and disposing memory and being cognizant of the uncertainty of this mortal life, do make and publish this my Last Will and Testament, and do by these presents hereby revoke any previous wills by me subscribed. First, I direct that all my just debts including burial expenses, be paid by my Executor hereinafter named. Second, I bequeath and devise to Megan Alvarez Grant and Daniel McClure, and to their respective heirs, successors and assigns forever, all of my land and real estate wheresoever situated, including the three sections of land leased by the Bar G ranch in Bobcat County, Nebraska, to hold said real estate in fee simple absolute as tenants in common.

"Third, I bequeath and give to Megan Alvarez Grant, all of my personal effects, horses, cattle, and residue of my property, to have and to hold the same unto said Megan Alvarez Grant, and her heirs and assigns forever."

The lawyer paused and wiped at his brow again, looking uncertainly at Megan across the desk. Lucas Battie would glean nothing from Megan Grant's expression, Dan thought, for it was still passive, almost disinterested. He wondered if she was even hearing the lawyer's words.

The lawyer continued reading. "Fourth, I nominate and appoint Daniel McClure as Executor of this my Last Will and Testament, and I authorize and empower him to do all things necessary to execute the terms and conditions of this Will. In witness whereof, I have hereunto put my hand this 28th day of June, 1882."

Battie placed the crisp parchment paper on his desk and leaned back in his chair. "The document is signed 'Solomon George Pyle'. My law clerk, Mr. Stone, and I subscribed as witnesses. I might say it is an exceptionally simple document, but Mr. Pyle insisted upon simplicity. I can assure you it is all legal and valid. Do either of you have any questions? Miss Grant?"

Megan responded with a barely perceptible shake of her head.

"Mr. McClure?"

"I think not."

"You might wonder about the specification that the land is to be owned as tenants in common. This means you will own undivided interests, with the ability to pass your share of the property to your own heirs. Also, either of you can force a sale of the whole at any time. You cannot be forced to own it together." He turned to Dan. "Mr. McClure, Mr. Pyle placed a great deal of faith in you."

"I'll try to be worthy of it."

"Very well, I have some papers for both of you to sign, and then I will proceed with filing the will for probate. The two of you will have to appear at a hearing in about a month, but it will be quite routine, and I think there is nothing to be concerned about."

"Fine," Dan said, "we'll keep in touch, and if I have any questions, I'll stop in."

But why in God's name had Sol Pyle left him a half interest in the ranch land? They had become friends, yes, but they had only known each other a few months. He didn't need the land. He didn't want it. And still, Sol squeezed out his promise that he would see that the terms of the will would be carried out. His interest in the land was one of the terms. It just didn't make any sense, especially in light of Sol's confession of paternity.

And what did Megan think about it? Looking at her now, there was no way to tell. Was she angry? Did she resent it? He had come to the Pine Ridge for peace and solitude. Day by day, this life was becoming more turbulent and complex. But he still was not leaving the Pine Ridge.

Dan assisted Megan into the carriage that the ranch hands had dusted off and pulled out of the barn for the journey to Medicine Hill. "You're a real dude, McClure, when you're all gussied up," came a grating voice from across the dusty trail that was Medicine Hill's main street.

Stiles Keaton stepped off the boardwalk and swaggered across the street toward the carriage. "High class transportation," the sheriff said mockingly, nodding at the carriage. He stopped not far from Dan, and his dark eyes fastened on Megan. "High class lady, too."

Megan sat unmoving, seemingly unhearing like a statue in the carriage.

"I was planning to pay you a visit before I left town," Dan said.

The sheriff arched his dark eyebrows and turned to Dan. "Oh?"

"I assume you've heard about the killings out at the Hannah Baker place."

"Rumors, that's all I've heard. Nothing official."

"Then I'll make it official. Hannah Baker and Solomon Pyle were murdered there, in cold blood."

"Is that right? I'd better look into it. And when did these alleged murders take place?"

"Sunday morning."

"And it's Tuesday afternoon. Why didn't you report them earlier?"

"Would it have made a difference?"

"It might have. The trail's cold by now. I'll ride out, but I probably won't find much."

"You probably won't," Dan said.

"I don't like your tone, mister."

"And I don't like your law, Sheriff. You don't seem to get very excited about killings in your county."

"Nobody's proved there was a murder. Folks get killed for a lot of reasons. Self-defense, for instance. The law even says there's justifiable killings. A whore like the widow Baker might give somebody good cause, and a cowboy sticking his pecker in a briar patch can get it taken off accidental like. A man with horse sense thinks twice about who he keeps company with. There's a lesson there for you, McClure, and I won't charge you a dollar for it."

"What are you suggesting, Sheriff?"

"Don't play the innocent lamb with me, McClure. Liz Dunkirk, that's what I'm suggesting. There's talk about you keeping company with her. You might as well jump in bed with a den of rattlesnakes. You're playing a mighty dangerous game, McClure, and I'll tell you something else . . . you're bound to lose."

"I see," Dan said, turning away from the sheriff and climbing into the buggy.

"Yes," the sheriff said, "we'll see . . . and soon, unless I miss my guess." He grinned like a Cheshire cat and pulled a cigar from his shirt pocket.

Dan took the reins and released the carriage brake, and without casting Sheriff Keaton so much as a glance, he snapped the reins and drove the buggy away.

The carriage rolled and bounced its way up the rocky rutted road that twisted into the foothills north of Medicine Hill. The ride back to the Bar G would take the better part of two hours, and Dan decided to concede Megan the silence she was maintaining. It might be wiser to say nothing than the wrong thing. Leave her with her thoughts. Give her time to sort things out. That's what he would have wanted himself at a time like this. Experience told him to keep his lips tight.

An hour out of Medicine Hill, Dan turned the horses off the road so they could get a drink at a clear spring-fed creek that raced down the slope alongside the roadbed. He had just stepped down from the carriage to water the horses when Megan spoke.

"This is Antelope Creek, isn't it?" she asked.

"I don't know the name. I'm a greenhorn in these parts, remember?"

"It's so cool here. We're in the shade. The trees are birch, aren't they?"

"Yes," he said, surprise showing in his voice.

"I know the place. Sol always stopped here, too. That's strange, isn't it?"

"It's a natural watering place."

"There should be a huge granite stone along the edge of the creek with kind of a round, flat top. I always called it Pancake Rock. It almost looked like someone carved it that way. Do you see it?"

Dan scanned the creek bank. It was amazing she knew where they were. "Yes, I see it. You couldn't mistake it."

Her lips parted in a smile that made him think of Emily on the Christmas before she died when she found a little rag doll under the Christmas tree.

"When we stopped here, I always used to get down and yank off my boots and sit on old Pancake Rock and soak my feet. The water's ice cold even in the heat of July. The creek's spring-fed. Sol would nag at me to hurry up, but I never paid any attention. I'd just sit there in the shade, listen to the meadowlarks, and watch the minnows in the creek."

Dan had a sudden inspiration. "Would you like to get down and soak your feet right now?"

"Are you serious?"

"Why not?"

"Well, my stockings . . . I'd have to take my stockings off."

"Then take them off," Dan said.

"But . . . you wouldn't look?"

He shook his head in disbelief. "No, I won't look."

"But how will I know?"

"Don't you trust me?"

She was silent a moment and her brow wrinkled thoughtfully. "Yes . . . yes, I do." Then her face flushed a bit. "Besides, you wouldn't see a thing you haven't already seen, would you?"

Recalling the night of Megan's injury, Dan replied, "That's true, but I'll behave honorably. I promise." He hurried around to her side of the carriage and took her hand. "I'll help you over to the rock, then you can take off those awful high-button shoes and your stockings while I water the horses."

After the horses had drunk their fill, Dan led them into the shade, braked the carriage, and secured the reins. When he joined Megan, she was positioned on the rock, her face serene and tilted skyward. Her skirt and petticoat were hiked up mid-thigh; her feet dangled lazily in the water where the current splashed around her shapely calves and ankles. She turned her head when she heard him step up behind her.

"Would you rather be alone?" he asked. "I would un-derstand."

"No, I think we should talk."

He let himself down on the ground next to the rock and then sat there waiting for her to speak.

"We'll have to arrive at some arrangement for Sol's land," she said, "now that you own half of it. Bar G cattle are grazing on it. Sol didn't have more than a few head of his own. I would hope to buy out your interest in the land someday, but I can't now. I'd like to keep leasing, if we can come to terms. Of course, I know you have a right to force a sale if you want."

He looked up at her. She had a determined look on her face, but he knew she was concerned. "It won't be sold," he said, "unless I sell it to you. I'll lease my interest to the Bar G on the same basis Sol did."

"It wasn't business with Sol," she said. "He took enough of the calf crop every year to pay the taxes. That was about it."

"That's good enough for me."

"No, we have to handle this in a businesslike way. You're a very poor businessman, you know."

"Yes, I know. You've told me that before. Why don't you handle this part of my business for me? I'll go along with whatever you think is right."

"No, you shouldn't."

"Can't I trust you?" he asked.

"Well, yes, but—"

"Then it's settled. You're my business manager."

"But you're Sol's executor."

"And as executor, I can delegate my responsibilities."

"Oh."

"Megan, all of Sol's land should have been yours. I had no idea he was going to do this. I don't understand why. We'd known each other such a short time."

"Sol thought very highly of you. I know that. He had his reasons. He always had a reason for everything he did, and he was almost always right . . . but I never told him that. I never told him a lot of things."

"Then you're not upset because he left part of the land to me?"

"No, of course not. As Mr. Battie explained before we left, if Sol hadn't made out a will, the land would have gone to the state, and I'm sure Dunkirk would have found a way to get hold of it then. I didn't have a right to inherit anything. Besides, an inheritance isn't a God-given right. It's one of the extras that some of us are fortunate enough to receive." She paused. "But I'd much rather have my father and Sol back than to have the inheritances I got from them. I know this, I'm not going to waste away what they left me. That would be an insult to their memories. I'm going to build on what they gave me."

Megan Grant was a damn tough lady.

"Dan, there's something else. How do we stop the killing? How do we deal with Dunkirk? I can run a ranch; I know that; I'm a good businesswoman. But I don't know how to fight a war."

"I was a soldier," Dan said. "I didn't like it, but I can soldier again if I have to. You handle the ranching business; I'll handle the war."

"But you won't have the law on your side. Sheriff Keaton works for Dunkirk. You can't doubt that, can you?"

"No, but I've written to the Attorney General's office. I'm hoping that eventually they'll send someone out here to look into things. Of course, there aren't many votes in Bobcat County, so I won't count on it. We'd better work out a strategy of our own."

"Keaton's a dangerous man, and he hates you, Dan. I hear things in people's voices that I didn't hear before and that other people don't hear. He plans to kill you."

"Not if Clay Sutherly has anything to say about it. He wants that privilege."

She bit her lower lip as if trying to hold back something she wanted to say. "I didn't know you'd met Elizabeth Dunkirk," she said.

"Uh, yes, we've met."

"It's none of my concern, of course, but the sheriff seemed to think you were more than casual acquaintances."

"She's dropped by the ranch a few times," Dan said, "to look at my paintings." It wasn't a total lie. She had seen the paintings on each of her half dozen visits to his place over the past month. She had to walk past some of his better works on the way to the bed.

"She's interested in your work then?"

"Yes, I guess you could say that." Dan had to get away from this subject fast. He did not owe Megan Grant an explanation about any relationship he had with Elizabeth Dunkirk, but somehow when he was with Megan he felt like he owed her one. She made him feel guilty as hell. It would probably last until Elizabeth showed up and he looked into her lustful, seductive eyes again. No, there were times for choosing. He was coming to such a time soon.

"Elizabeth Dunkirk's a very beautiful woman," Megan said.

"Yes, I suppose she is in some ways. Megan, we'd probably better be on our way if we want to get back to the Bar G before sundown." He stood up. "We should talk about tomorrow's meeting on the way back."

"Yes, I suppose. There's not much more to talk about since you don't want to talk about Elizabeth Dunkirk and her interest . . . in your art, of course."

Chapter 18

MEGAN SAT AT the head of the oak dining table that her father had hauled to the Pine Ridge all the way from Texas. She was not as uncomfortable as she had thought she might be. Their conversation had been subdued during dinner, and the ranchers had treated her deferentially as they displayed their cowboy appetites on the rare roast beef, hot biscuits and fresh gooseberry pies that had been placed on the table. Now they were washing it down with hot coffee.

If she could only see them. There was still too much hidden from her ears and that other indefinable sense that had been growing with each new day. If her eyesight ever returned, she would view the countryside and the creatures and the people around her with new reverence and appreciation, she vowed.

Besides Dan, who sat at Megan's right, there were five ranchers of varying ages, circumstances, and temperaments in the room. Caleb Salway, pot-bellied, but bronzed and vigorous, well past 60, was both the oldest and best fixed of the small ranchers. He was also soft-spoken and level-headed, one who'd say little, but whose words would come down heavy.

Tom Powell, in his mid-20's, not much older than herself, owned only a section and leased another two. He was always stretched for cash and was the bullheaded sort. He was not as tall as Dan, but thicker boned. Sol had always said that young Tom had a herd bull's neck and shoulders, and once she had heard Sol remark to a hand, when he had not been aware she was listening, that young Tom had a herd bull's balls to boot. He was married and kept his young wife perpetually with child.

But the area ranchers, more especially their wives and daughters, knew him more as a fence jumper who ran helter-skelter through the Pine Ridge. More than once, she had felt Tom Powell stripping her naked with his eyes, and she supposed he was doing it now since she could not look back. She wondered vaguely if she had blushed at the thought of it. But Tom had his following as he had his detractors, and he would command the support of some good fighting men.

The other men, Cap Morris of the Rocking M, Chris Tyler of the Tumbling T and Lem Stack, were a blend of the two extremes, but would lean to the cooler head of Cal Salway in an argument. It didn't matter. She had decided to concede them nothing; not her age; not her handicap; not her femaleness. She owned the Bar G, and with the land she leased from Sol's estate and Dan, she controlled more land than any man in the room. She had as much stake in the Pine Ridge as any of them.

Reminding herself of this, she spoke, her voice clear and steady. "Gentlemen, I thank you for coming. You were invited here today to discuss a mutual problem. I don't have to tell you what we're faced with this summer. Three have died already this year. How many others in the past? As you know, a man tried unsuccessfully to kill me, and Mr. McClure here was shot in the back several months ago. We have no law in this county right now, only Woodson Dunkirk. The Diamond D is the law. And if we don't do something about it, the Diamond D is going to eat up the county before this is all over. Our family burial plots are going to be overcrowded, and Diamond D cows will be pasturing over the graves of our loved ones. I can't see anyone in this room; I can't see the cows grazing in the meadows, but I can see the future. If we don't make a decision today that this is going to stop and that we're going to fight back, do you know what I see in the future? I see us being trampled in the Pine Ridge dust by Diamond D riders." There was a rumble of assent in the room.

Megan continued, "I'm just reminding you of what you already know. I can't force you to do anything about them, but I can tell you right now I'm not going to sit on my fanny and wait for Dunkirk to burn out the Bar G. Or to send his gunslingers over to finish the job on me that they botched up before. I'm going to fight back. I think Dan McClure will help me . . . will help all of us . . . if you'll back him. Let me say this . . . Mr. McClure and I have our differences, and he still needs some educating about some things around here. But he's got his own stake in this. Most of you know he owns the Hanson place. What you probably don't know is that he owns half of another three sections that Sol Pyle leased to the Bar G." The stunned silence told Megan that the ranchers' curiosity had been whetted. She decided to let it go unsatisfied. "Dan has a military background. He graduated from West Point, and he fought the Sioux. We need a leader who can plan and organize and carry the fight to the enemy."

If she could just see their faces. She could not gauge their reaction as to whether they were hostile or friendly to her suggestion.

"Unlike the rest of us, Dan doesn't know most of the ranchers around here. At first I thought that might be a problem, but now I don't think so. He's in a position to start fresh. He doesn't have to overcome any old grudges or feuds. He can make hard-nosed decisions without the fear of offending an old friend, not that it would matter to him anyway."

"How about getting to the point, Meg? I've got work to get back to," Tom Powell interrupted.

"Very well. I want you and the rest of the men to join the Bar G and Dan in this fight. If you will, we can whip Dunkirk. If you won't, he'll chop us down, one by one."

"Sounds to me like you're taking it upon yourself to appoint a goddamned general," Powell growled. "I know you've been through a lot, but that don't give you the right to start settin' terms for the rest of us."

"I'm not setting terms. I'm telling you what I intend to do, and I'm inviting you to join me."

"But you can see Tom's point."

She recognized Cap Morris's drawl. Sol always said Cap had a voice like a rusty gate hinge.

"It's kind of hard to see why your notions should carry more weight than anyone else's," he added.

"Because I'm a woman?"

"Well, it goes a little against a man's grain. But not just that. Meaning no disrespect, I know'd you when you was a little girl, and that wasn't so long ago. It goes down a little hard when you're up there telling us what we ought to do."

It was Cal Salway's deep, mellow voice next. "I think we ought to hear what Mr. McClure has to say."

That decided it. The ranchers fell silent.

"I'll be more than glad to tell you what I had in mind," Dan said. "You don't know me, and I don't know you, but I hope that's going to change very quickly. Megan's told you about my background. You can decide for yourselves what that's worth. There is one other thing I have to offer, and that's time. All of you have ranches to run. You've got work you ought to be tending to right now. All of my land is under lease. I can leave my work for a time, although reluctantly, without great harm."

"Just what kind of work is it that you do?" Tom Powell asked, his voice hostile.

"I'm a painter . . . an artist."

Silent disapproval hung heavy in the room. Dan had weakened his case with that admission, Megan thought, and she felt a rising tide of anger at the prejudice of her rancher friends until she recalled that they reflected doubts that she, too, once had.

Dan continued, "Let me tell you what I think we should do. Then you can ask yourselves if there is a man here who can make the time to plan and organize an army. At this point I have to speak in generalities, but somehow I want to establish, beyond any doubt, who's responsible for these raids."

Tom Powell interjected. "Hell, if you ain't got that figured out, mister, you can't do us no good."

"I know everything points to the Diamond D," Dan said, "but who at the Diamond D? Woodson Dunkirk? Or is it Sutherly? Where exactly does Sheriff Keaton fit in? Somebody used the word 'general'. Well, that's what we've got to do here . . . know for sure who their general is before we try to whip his army. Beyond that, there are some things I'd like to see done as soon as possible. You've got places on these ridges that overlook half the county. Men like we're dealing with ride mostly under the cover of dark and generally attack between sundown and shortly after sunrise. I want to establish a series of watch posts during those hours. We'll station men at strategic places and work out a signal system. If they see fire or smoke or some other sign of trouble, they can alert the other ranchers and hopefully, we can get help to the parties in trouble. If we can spare the men, I think we should consider night patrol. At the very least, deploy scouts along the roads leading from the Diamond D headquarters. I'd like to divide the valley into four or five areas with a commander designated for each and have the ranchers and cowhands in each area organized so they can ride at a moment's notice. But the important thing is for someone to be in charge and to have a plan of action."

"I can't guess who that might be," Powell said sarcastically.

Dan ignored the comment. "We continue to lose valuable time sitting around waiting for the next strike, hoping it will be somebody else's place. Defending the ranches in the Pine Ridge should be our primary objective, but once we're organized we can develop a plan to smoke these raiders out, maybe set a trap and spring it. I don't want to live in a county that's protected by vigilante committees for the next ten years any more than I want to live in a place that's run by one man's law. I don't think any of you do, either. But one way or another, we've got to bring a halt to the raids and killings. We might find good reason to continue our organization for other purposes over the years, but that's something we can discuss later. After we put our guns away. That's pretty much it, gentlemen."

"And where do we fit into this?" Cal asked.

"From what Charlie Gates says, your ranches are pretty well scattered over the valley. You would be logical area commanders, but a few of you might fit somewhere else. That all has to be worked out, hopefully, yet this afternoon, if you want to be counted in. Certainly, you are the men who will have to get the word to the other ranchers. You were asked to come here because it was felt that you had the respect of your friends and neighbors. I'm a stranger. You're naturally skeptical about anything I have to say. I have to convince you before we can look to other support."

"You can't organize the ranchers in these parts," Powell said. "I ain't sayin' your notion's so bad. Landowners hereabouts have been feudin' and fussin' amongst themselves too long. But, hell, you got about as much chance as a grasshopper in an anthill of getting the Pine Ridge ranchers to go along with something like this."

"Tom's right," Lem Stack drawled. "Ranchers are an independent bunch. That's why they sink their roots in this Godforsaken country. They like working alone, being their own bosses."

"How can a man be his own boss," Dan countered, "if Woodson Dunkirk ends up with his ranch? A dead man doesn't have much say."

"Even if we go along with this idea of yours, McClure, folks around here wouldn't go for a stranger ramrodding the operation," Stack said.

"That's fine," Dan said. "I'm not looking for a job. I'd be more than happy to let somebody else take charge. I just want you to know I'm willing to do it. But you know your people best. I'll put it in your hands, and I'll play whatever role you want me to. But even if you don't want any part of it, Megan and I don't intend to lie down and play dead for the Diamond D. We'll go it alone."

"You're sayin' we're yellar?" Powell said.

"No, of course not. I respect your rights to make your own decisions. My natural inclination is to sit back and hope that this is the end of it. But I've been following my natural inclination since I was shot, since the night Megan was injured, and in that time, three people have been killed."

"I ain't backing away from a fight," Powell said. "Me and my hired men have been packin' a lot of hardware these past weeks, but I don't know that you're the man to tell us when and who to start shootin'."

Megan heard Caleb Salway, who sat to her left, scoot his chair back on the hard oak floor. "I got a long way to ride gents. I got to be on my way. Count me in, McClure. If you want, I'll work the ranchers north of Beaver Creek.

I think most of the boys in that part of the county will see it your way. We don't need but one general. Figure out your plans; get word to me what you want done." Salway stood. "I thank you for the invite, Miss Megan. You set a mighty fine table. More than that, you do a real credit to your pa and old Sol. We need more ranchers hereabouts with your kind of grit and horse sense."

Taken aback somewhat, Megan smiled weakly. "Thank you, Cal. Thanks for everything." She heard the clack of the salty rancher's boots as he ambled across the floor and walked out the door.

A dead silence consumed the room for a moment after Caleb Salway's departure. "Oh, what the hell," Lem Stack growled. "What have we got to lose? I'll ride with you a ways, McClure."

"Yeah, me too," Tom Powell said. "As long as it's understood that I pull out if I don't like the way things are going."

"That's understood," Dan said. "I wouldn't expect anyone to do otherwise."

An hour later, when the four remaining ranchers rode away from the Bar G, the foundation of the Pine Ridge Cattlemen's Association had been laid.

Chapter 19

IT WAS MID-MORNING when Dan bolted upright in bed at the sound of the soft rapping at his door. He rubbed the back of his neck, groggily thinking he had been dreaming. He heard the knocking again.

"Dan, are you in there?"

Damn, it was Liz. Not today. He wasn't ready to deal with her yet. "Yeah, just a minute. I'm in bed. I'm not dressed yet."

"That's all right," she said teasingly. "Don't get dressed on my account."

Dan swung his long legs off the bed and reached for the faded denim trousers that were draped across the chair. He had slept a drugged sleep last night. He could not remember the last time he had not been up with the sun. Sol's death; the meeting with the lawyer; the confrontation with the ranchers; it must all be wearing on him more than he had realized. He felt like he'd been trampled by a buffalo herd this morning, and now he had to start the day by facing up to Liz Dunkirk.

He buckled up his britches as he padded barefoot to the door and opened it. She stood there, facing him, her golden mane shining in the morning sun, her devilish blue eyes betraying the feigned pout formed by her full lips. Her alluring fragrance and the sight of her clad in violet riding garb, tailored precisely to her full and statuesque figure, exposing her tantalizing cleavage, overpowered him, and the hunger surged in him again, threatening to tear down his resolve.

She pushed by and marched into the house, brandishing her riding crop in her hand like a royal scepter. He shrugged and closed the door, and as he followed her into the room, he noticed that her eyes were casting about suspiciously before she turned to him.

"You took long enough," she said.

"I told you I was in bed."

"I thought you had company."

"You obviously thought wrong."

She placed her riding crop on the table and stepped to him, placing one hand tentatively on his bare waist, running the slender fingers of the other through his curly, sandy chest hair, raking, combing and smoothing, like a woman might caress a pet cat. She was wise in the ways of seduction, almost as astute as Angela, he thought. But Angela had been a professional.

What Liz lacked was Angela's warmth and humanity. On second thought, perhaps Liz Dunkirk should be ranked with the professionals, for a man who dallied with Liz's kind paid a price in more than dollars. And Dan had an uneasy feeling she had come to submit her bill.

"I told you that you didn't have to get dressed on my account," she purred, her hand slithering down his belly and coming to rest on his belt buckle.

Maybe they could talk later, he tried to convince himself as his arousal heightened. No, the lines were being drawn in more ways than one. It was time for choosing. He had decided several years back how he was going to spend the rest of his life, and Liz Dunkirk could only get in the way of those plans. She had only one thing he wanted, but there were other—more important—things, in life. Liz was like a festering boil on his butt; he wouldn't rest easy till he got her out of his system.

He moved away from her, leaving her standing there, the expression on her face disbelieving. He searched out a shirt and pair of socks, averting her gaze as he slipped on the shirt and sat down on the edge of the bed to pull on his boots. After he finished dressing, he looked up. She stood where he had left her, hands planted on her hips, staring at him with cold eyes, her lips pursed tight.

He rose and moved toward her. "We'd better talk," he said.

"So it would appear."

He gestured toward the table. "Shall we sit down? Have a cup of coffee?"

"I think not. I have the distinct feeling I'm not welcome here."

"It's not that. I've enjoyed the times we spent together." He was trying to choose his words carefully.

She turned away from him. "I should think so. Now you'll be able to tell your friends about your tumbles in the hay with Miss Dunkirk."

"I think you're a better judge of character than that, Liz. Whatever happened between us is our private business."

"May I ask why you're casting me aside like this?"

"Don't play the woman scorned, Liz . . . it doesn't become you. You've come to our . . . our little rendezvous with more than your share of enthusiasm, but I never felt you attached any more significance to our relationship than I did. We found pleasure in each other, nothing more. It would have ended sooner or later."

"Why now?" she asked.

"I can't say."

"I know about the Pine Ridge Cattlemen's Association. I know you're heading it up. Does it have something to do with that?"

Dunkirk knew already. And in less than 24 hours. That placed a new urgency on the work to be done. If the Diamond D meant business—and he was quite certain it did—there would be more strikes against the valley ranchers in an effort to diffuse the Association's attempts to organize resistance.

"Yes, that's a part of it. It seems likely that the Association and the Diamond D are going to be on opposite sides. I think it would be a little awkward if we continued to see each other under the circumstances."

She turned to face him again, her face calm and impassive.

"You're a fool, Dan. We could be on the same side."

"I doubt it."

"I've asked you to kill Clay Sutherly several times."

"I'm not a hired gun. And anyway, I didn't take it seriously."

"But I was serious. I hate Clay Sutherly. I'll be nothing but a slave if he acquires control of the Diamond D. By marriage or otherwise. I want him dead. Then Daddy will listen to me."

"You want the empire for yourself, is that it?"

"Frankly, yes. And Clay Sutherly stands in my way. If you kill him, Dan, you'll solve all your problems. He's behind the killings, not Daddy. Oh, Daddy wants the ranches. He wants your place in the worst way, and the Bar G, and most of the others in the valley. But killing's not his way. He would find a way to take them if he was calling the moves. But physically, he's too weak, so he's leaving it all in Clay's hands."

"Then you're admitting that the Diamond D's responsible for the killings and burnings?"

"Clay Sutherly is, not the Diamond D. And the gunslingers he's hired. If I had my say, I'd fire them all . . . after I had Sutherly killed."

"Why don't you go to the law?"

"Daddy would never forgive me. And besides, I hate to bring Sheriff Keaton into this. It's a family matter. Can't you see how easy it could be? You could do it. You're one man who could do it."

"It's not that simple. I don't kill men because somebody asks me to. I'm not a gun for hire, and I'm beginning to understand that's what you had in mind from the beginning. You thought you were hiring a gun."

She seemed unfazed by the innuendo that she was no more than a prostitute. She walked over to the table and picked up her riding crop and toyed with it in her hand for a few moments before speaking. "You could marry me, Dan. Daddy would have to change his plans then. We'd have to get married right away, before Daddy or Sutherly could interfere."

"I don't believe what I'm hearing."

"I'm quite serious."

"But I don't love you, and I don't believe for one moment that you love me."

"I'll be totally truthful with you," she said. "No, I don't love you, at least not in any especially sentimental way. But I'm looking for marriage. I want a strong man, one who complements my own personality. Think about it, Dan. You could do worse. You can't deny that we satisfy certain needs that a man and woman have. And I am fond of you." Her eyes roamed up and down the length of his body. "I think we could make strong, intelligent children together. A solid new generation to take over the Diamond D someday. And your work . . . you could pursue your painting without financial worries. I know nothing of art, and I don't care to know more, but I would think that our financial resources could be useful in acquiring the fame I assume you seek. I would tend to the day to day operation of the ranch; that's my dream. That's where my fulfillment is." Her eyes met his. "Now, does this seem so absurd?"

"No, not entirely," he admitted. "It might appeal to a lot of men. It would be like being put out to stud, so to speak. But I don't find it very appealing. I'm afraid my pride is such that I want whatever talent I have to provide any recognition I achieve, as well as any financial success I have. And I want to love the woman I marry. I had that experience once, and I want it again. I won't settle for less. And I'm looking for a partner in the woman I marry. I don't want to be her pet husband, and I don't want her to be my pet wife."

"Your idealism makes me nauseous," she said.

"Then perhaps you'd better go. The fresh air might help."

She started to turn away but then hesitated. "I'm curious," she said.

"About what?"

"You've found that woman you're talking about, haven't you?"

"No. What makes you think so?"

"The things you've said. You know too well the kind of woman you want to spend your life with. She's already there. Somewhere in the back of your mind. Is it that young Grant woman? She doesn't seem much more than a child. Of course, I haven't seen her for some time. She always seemed such a wild creature. I suppose a man might find her beautiful in an exotic sort of way. Is she the one?"

"I've never thought about her in that way."

"You will." She smiled knowingly.

"Somehow, you just don't look like a gypsy fortune teller," he said.

"Just wait and see."

She extended her hand, and Dan took it in his own. "I shall miss you, Dan, but I wish you well. And I give you my thanks, because I think you will still help my cause in spite of yourself."

"Good luck, Liz, and I wish you well, too." He released her hand and watched her as she turned away and jauntily walked out of the house.

As he heard her horse gallop away, it occurred to him that he had liked her better in those last moments than he had at any time during their most frenzied romp. She was a formidable woman. Life with her would have been anything but dull . . . and anything but happy. Then he remembered what she had said. Clay Sutherly knew about the Cattlemen's Association. Damn. He couldn't waste another day. He had better ride out and call upon the area captains, perhaps scout out some signal posts. He had a feeling time was running short.

Chapter 20

I T WAS WELL past midnight when Dan reined the strawberry roan mare onto the trail that led over the ridge that divided his land from Megan Grant's. The mare, which he had borrowed from the Bar G, was fresh and strong in the unseasonable cool night air. His own horse had been blowing hard and limping on a tender front leg when Dan had dismounted and walked it the last half mile to Megan's ranch. He had scared the hell out of them when he had led the horse into the ranch yard a little more than an hour earlier. At least Megan had had the good sense to post a guard on the veranda of the limestone-walled house. Sol's nondescript old hound, though, had started howling like he had a coon treed when Dan had reached the fringes of the farmstead, and the kid keeping watch on the porch had displayed a nervous trigger finger and fired off a wild shot before Dan identified himself and walked into the open. Within seconds, Charlie Gage, who had taken up residence in Sol's old room, burst out of the house clad only in his long johns with his six-gun probing the air, looking for a target. Dan smiled now at the thought of the old man standing there on the porch ready to take on the whole Sioux nation if he had to in the defense of Megan Grant. Long John Charlie, they called him, for he wore red flannels winter and summer. Sometimes when you rode downwind from the old bird you had to wonder if he always wore the same pair.

Nate Coates and the other hands had come rushing up from the bunkhouse. Poor Nate, what the kid wouldn't give to have Charlie's bed in the main house . . . or to share Megan Grant's.

Megan had a rare, indefinable quality that bred instant loyalty. Even when her quick temper and sometimes razor-sharp tongue made you want to give her a quick whack on the butt, you never felt like walking away from her. He was not sure what he felt for Megan Grant, but loyalty had something to do with it and that was no small part of the reason he and Liz Dunkirk had parted company.

Damn, Megan Grant. She had made him weak in his knees when she had appeared in the doorway tonight. And it wasn't because he was saddle sore and dead tired from the gauntlet-like ride from ranch to ranch through the Pine Ridge this day. She had stood there, the moonlight casting an eerie glow on her face, her unseeing eyes bright and alert. He should not have been surprised, for why should he expect to see the strong-willed and fiercely independent Megan Grant surrender to the demands of custom and style and adorn herself in a frilly, appropriately modest nightdress? No, she had stood there in an old flannel shirt that had sheared-off sleeves and stopped well above her knees, showing too much of her brown shapely legs. Her good sense had stopped her before she stepped out onto the porch in that outfit.

Dan had seen the longing in Nate Coate's eyes as he stood in front of the porch, his mouth gaping open in awe. Then he had observed the hurt in the young man's eyes when she invited Dan in for coffee before he rode on. Charlie had instructed one of the hands to saddle up a fresh horse and to look after Dan's own exhausted mount before he limped off to bed, leaving Dan and Megan alone in the kitchen where Megan, with seemingly little effort, brewed a pot of coffee on the stove that still had hot coals in its belly from the evening's supper.

Dan sat at the table, watching her silently, as she took two cups from the cupboard and placed them on the table. She must have somehow sensed his gaze, he thought, when she said, "You'll have to forgive my attire. It was the only thing handy." Her face had suddenly blushed scarlet when she realized the implication of what she had said.

He smiled at her discomfort, letting the silence speak for itself as she turned abruptly away to move to the stove. "The coffee should be ready," she said.

"Thank you for your trouble."

"No trouble. I'd do the same for anybody." She placed the pot on the table and sat down across from Dan. "Perhaps you'd better pour," she said. "I'm a little clumsy at that yet."

Dan took the pot and filled their cups with steaming coffee. "Thank you for not coddling me," she said as she reached for her cup, touching it tentatively before enclosing it in her slender fingers.

"I don't understand."

"Everyone around here treats me like a child. Charlie and Nate are like a couple of old mother hens. They mean well, but it upsets me the way they stumble over each other trying to help me. They don't think I can do anything for myself. You aren't like that. In fact, you're just the opposite. Sometimes you let me do things I'd just as soon let somebody else do, but at least you don't treat me like a child."

"You're not a child. Far from it. But be patient with Nate and Charlie. You're lucky to have them. And your other hands; they're good men. They'll stick by you come hell or high water, and from the commotion that was raised out there when I showed up, I feel a lot better about things. I don't think anybody's going to take the Bar G by surprise."

"But what about your place?" she asked, before suddenly changing the subject. "By the way, you've never named your ranch or given it a brand. We can't just go on calling it the Hanson place forever."

"There's no hurry. Maybe it won't need a name or a brand."

"You're thinking of leaving?"

He caught the concern in her voice. "No. I said before I wasn't leaving. I meant it. I'm just not in a hurry to tag it with a name."

"But I do worry," she said. "You have to sleep sometime, and you're there alone. It's dangerous for you to stay there like that. I could send one of my hands over to stay nights, and you could sleep in shifts."

"No, that's not necessary. I'll be all right. Things will be a lot safer in the valley in a few days. I talked to Cal Salway and Powell and the other captains. They've already been at work, and they're going to make more contacts tomorrow. By tomorrow night, we'll have seven watch posts manned at the highest points of Pine Ridge. At first sign of trouble, someone will ride for help. By this time next week, we'll have patrols riding the trails at night."

"But you have hundreds of square miles of hills and valleys to cover," Megan reminded. "It won't take all that much skill to get past your patrols."

"No, but with scouts working around the Diamond D and relay riders at strategic places, we can get word of trouble to the watch stations and move men quickly with signal fires. We'll have armed men ready to strike, and we'll improve our odds of dealing Dunkirk's riders a blow. We'll certainly get help faster to the people who need it. I have a hunch that eventually we'll have to carry the fight to the Diamond D, but I haven't come up with the right plan yet. But I will."

He had left Megan Grant's kitchen reluctantly. It was a comfortable place to be. It was nice to share a table with a woman. Sometimes, nicer than sharing a bed.

They talked easily now. He and Megan weren't like a pair of bulldogs fighting over a bone anymore. They could speak frankly, yet amiably, with each other, like old friends, and he had a hard time now recollecting what they had ever argued about.

Chapter 21

REACHING THE TOP of the ridge, Dan stopped for a moment while he looked out over the starlit valleys that weaved between the twisting hills and ridges and widened and converged into great flatlands before, like spokes off a hub, they angled in all directions before they split off into the hills again. They talked about the ranchers in the valley, Dan thought, but in reality the Pine Ridge was a network of many grass-carpeted valleys, protected and bordered by rocky hills and ridges rich with ponderosa and ash and oak. God's country, the cowboys said, as they called ranch country everywhere. Dan agreed. Whatever God there was above, he felt closer to Him here than in any church he ever frequented.

Suddenly, his body tensed in the saddle. Through the trees, he caught the sight of a tiny, almost imperceptible glow of orange flickering like a candle in a draft. It was his place, and it wasn't a candle. He slapped the roan on the rump and reined her down the rocky trail that wound down the slope floor of his own small valley. He pushed the horse harder than he should have down the trail. Several times before they broke off the slope and onto the meadow, the game mare lost her footing and pitched forward, almost throwing him off before she regained her balance.

Once out of the hills, Dan dug his heels into the mare's flanks and raced her across the meadow at a reckless gallop. The fiery glow grew brighter and lighter and higher as he neared the ranch buildings, confirming his worst fears. He could see now there were three distinct fires raging on the ranch; the largest would be the barn; the others the cow shed and house.

The house. His paintings. A lifetime's work. He urged the horse forward at a frantic gait now, and as he barreled down the road that led into the ranch yard, he saw three, perhaps four horseback raiders fleeing the ranch at breakneck speed. Then, as he burst into the ranch yard, he came upon two stragglers, one yanking sharply at the reins of a reluctant, fire-spooked horse. The other was afoot, trying to steady another panicky horse, trying to run without its rider.

Dan pulled the roan up short and reached for his revolver, which slid into his hand and was aimed at the bulky rider before the man caught sight of him and grappled for his own gun. The man's gun never cleared its holster, as Dan squeezed the trigger of the army Colt, and the bullet tore through the raider's throat and seemed to lift him from the saddle as his horse vaulted out from under him and dashed away, leaving its dead master in a heap on the dusty earth.

The other raider's six-gun appeared instantly in his hand, and he leveled off a quick shot before Dan could steady the roan and get off a shot of his own. The horse lunged forward, letting out a blood-curdling shriek that seemed almost human before it fell to the earth. Dan leaped free, landing next to the wounded mare and taking a jolting blow to his left shoulder. He then scrambled to his feet with the revolver poised in his right hand. The gunfighter's six-gun roared again, but the frantic jerking of his horse threw him off his mark, and before he could fire again, Dan's bullet dug into the man's hip. The bullet's impact drove the man reeling backward and he stumbled, releasing his horse's reins before he steadied himself. His eyes were dazed and stunned as he tried to focus on his target.

The bastard isn't a quitter, Dan thought, giving him grudging respect before his own gun exploded and drove a bullet into the man's chest. The raider's gun slid from his hand and dropped to the ground as the man's knees buckled and he sunk to the earth, collapsing not more than a few feet from his sidekick.

Dan holstered his pistol, his eyes taking in the scene. The house. The paintings. Flames raced up the side walls of the house and danced over the rooftop while black smoke billowed out the open door. But the doorway itself seemed clear of fire. Was there a chance he could still salvage the paintings?

He raced for the house, oblivious to the searing heat that had turned the ranch yard into a broiling oven. He pounded across the front porch and sucked in a deep breath before he bolted through the open entryway. Once inside, he knew instantly he was too late. One room had already been devoured by the vicious fire, and the paintings in this room had already been swallowed by the flames. He hesitated for a dangerous moment, and almost blinded by the thick stinging smoke, surveyed the room with tear-filled eyes.

Then he remembered Sol's portrait. He had left it near the door, planning to take it to Megan's the first chance he got, feeling that somehow it belonged on the Bar G, even if Megan couldn't see it. He wheeled, pulling the heavy smoke into his lungs as he tried to catch his breath. Choking and coughing, he staggered to the front wall where he found the canvas resting on the floor. He snatched it up and, clutching it protectively to his chest, Dan charged for the open doorway and broke out onto the porch. Only after he had stumbled across the yard and collapsed on the ground, gasping for breath, his stomach churning, was he aware of the pain where the flames had scorched his arms and face.

Then he heard the agonizing whinny of the roan. Looking across the yard, he saw the flailing legs and the strained jerking of the helpless mare's head and neck. He lifted himself up, and after depositing the rescued canvas on a soft bed of grass, he walked on trembling legs to the suffering horse. He looked down at her and saw that she had taken a bullet in the upper neck just behind the jaw. Her glazed eyes told him she was beyond help. He pulled the long barreled service revolver from its holster and ended the animal's misery.

He turned away from the dead horse and stopped, standing there and surveying the ranch yard totally illuminated now by the fiery blaze that had once been his home. He tried not to think of the three horses that had been in the barn, but the thought occurred to him that this was an odd breed of Westerner who fired a barn without turning out the horses.

His eyes were drawn to the house and the sounds of the creaking and crackling of the timbers just before the roof collapsed and sunk into the rooms that had housed his paintings. Ten years' harvest of a creative mind and skilled hands, cremated to ashes. His only tangible reminders of Larisa and Emily and Angela burned into the Pine Ridge dust.

The paintings, all of them, had been a part of him, children of his soul. And now they were nothing.

He began to shake spasmodically; his stomach knotted with a knifelike pain that ripped through his belly. He bent forward and began to cough and retch violently, before the dizziness struck and blackness overtook him, and he fell into his own vomit.

Chapter 22

THE PUNGENT ODOR of smoke struck Megan's nostrils long before they reached Dan's ranch and told her the story that would unfold there. One of the hands had sighted smoke shortly after sunrise and had carried word to the house, and the news had hit her with a sinking feeling in the pit of her stomach that lingered yet as she pondered what they might find when they rode into Dan McClure's ranch yard. There was a chance, just a chance, that Dan might have arrived home after the raiders hit the ranch, but if he had, why hadn't he returned to the Bar G for help? Not that there was much anyone could have done at that point.

They rode across the flatlands at a fast, steady gait: Megan, Nate Coates, and Charlie Gates. When she had announced she was riding with them, Charlie had grumbled and Nate had whined in protest, but she bristled and bluntly pulled rank. "Are you still working for me," she asked, "or do you want to draw your pay?"

Charlie had replied, "You're the boss, Miss Megan," and Nate just walked away and saddled his horse. Charlie didn't harbor grudges and had been a cowhand for years, taken too many orders to let one stick in his craw now.

But Nate had been quiet and sullen ever since they rode away from the Bar G. He was pouting again. He had been doing a lot of that lately. He still fancied that he would be ramrodding the Bar G one day as her husband. Well, he had better not take that for granted. Maybe he would; then again, maybe he would not. She was fond of Nate, grateful to him for his loyalty, appreciative of his affection, but there had been no more than a few quick, clumsy kisses passed between them, and when she thought about it, she had to admit that her feelings for Nate were more akin to what one might have for a kid brother than for a man she would want to spend a lifetime with. What Nate stirred in her was nothing compared to what she felt when in Dan McClure's presence. My God, what was she thinking?

Dan. She had resigned herself to the possibility that she might never see his face again. She could endure that thought, live with it. But now, she was faced with the prospect that she might never again hear the sound of his voice or tremble at the touch of his hand.

The smoke was heavy now, choking, suffocating, as they slowed their horses and trotted into the yard. "Charlie, what do you see?" Megan asked, as they reined in the horses. "Do you see Dan? Tell me."

"Nope. The roan's stretched out in the yard. Took some lead in the neck. It looks like somebody could have put her out of her misery. And she's got company. Two hombres is layin' there staring at the sky, but seeing nothin'. One of them I've seen riding with the Diamond D outfit. They didn't suffer none, that's for damn sure. Somebody sunk his bullets where they count."

"Dan?"

"It would be a good bet," Charlie said, "but don't get your hopes up, Miss Megan. There was a bunch of riders here last night."

She heard the creaking of Nate's saddle as he dismounted. "I'm going to take a look around," he said.

As Nate walked away, Megan said, "Tell me about it, Charlie. The buildings . . . is there anything left?"

"Not a golderned thing, Miss Megan. Ain't nothin' but smoke and ashes. The barn, the sheds, the house—"

"The house. What does the house look like?"

"Like I said, ashes. No, more like a big bed of cooking coals excepting for the chimney sticking out."

The sinking feeling hit her again. "The paintings. Dan's paintings."

"What's that, Miss Megan?"

"Nothing, Charlie." Little tears squeezed out of the corners of her eyes and began to trickle down her cheeks. You could rebuild a house or a barn; you could restock a ranch; but you could not replace Dan's paintings. The mood and emotions that gave birth to a particular painting had to be something you couldn't recapture and recreate again. Each painting would be like a child, each uniquely different and special, prized and cherished for that uniqueness. And just as irreplaceable as human life, if not as valued.

Dan, she prayed silently, *you have to be alive. You have to paint again.*

"Meg. Charlie," Nate called. "He's over here."

Megan turned to the sound of Nate's voice. "Is he—"

"He's all right," Nate said. "Leastways, he don't seem too bad."

Megan and Charlie dismounted, and Charlie led her around the smoldering embers of the house. "Nate's over by the trees west of the house," Charlie said as they walked. "There's McClure. He's just sitting there with his back against a ponderosa. Looks mighty worn out."

"He's alive. That's all that matters."

"He ain't very talkative," Nate said, walking toward them, "and he's damned ill-tempered. I asked him what we ought to do about them two gunslingers. You know what he said? He said 'roast the bastards,' begging your pardon, Meg."

"Nate, I think he's right," she replied. "We should roast the bastards."

Nate's silence spoke his disapproval and horror at her remarks.

"Dan," Megan called, "where are you?"

"Over here," he said. His voice was soft, but steady.

Charlie's hand closed gently around her arm. "This way, Miss Megan," he said as he led her in the direction of Dan's voice. "Would you like to sit down, ma'am?" Charlie asked when they neared Dan.

"Yes, I would, Charlie, thank you."

The cowhand helped her down to a pine-needle cushioned spot on the slope, and she positioned herself Indian-style there. She heard Dan's back brush against the loose ponderosa bark. He was no more than three or four feet to her left.

"Uh, Mr. McClure," Charlie stammered, "about them two pieces of buzzard bait out there in the yard, me and Nate can put 'em a few inches under if you'd like."

"I don't want them buried on my land," Dan said.

"Well, I reckon we could tote them over to the Bar G."

"I don't want them buried there either," Dan said.

"Then you're really fixin' to burn them up?"

"I was thinking about it, but no, I think we ought to send them home."

"Home?"

"To the Diamond D."

"I see . . . I guess," Charlie said.

"You'll probably find their horses in the trees north of what's left of the barn. If you would, I'd like you and Nate to haul the bodies to Caleb Salway's. Explain what happened and ask him to spread the word. See if he can spare a few hands to ride out to the Diamond D with you. I don't think you'll have any trouble in the daylight, but it wouldn't hurt to have a few extra guns. Just drop them off at the main gate. I think Dunkirk and Sutherly will get the message."

"Well, I guess we can do that all right . . . if it's okay with Miss Megan."

"I'd like you to do what he asked," she said.

"Well, then we'll tend to it right away."

"And something else, Charlie," Dan said.

"Tell Cal I want each captain in the Cattlemen's Association to have a patrol ready to ride. Let's see . . . not tomorrow night. The next night. I'll be in touch with the particulars."

"I'll do that, Mr. McClure." Then he added, "But if me and Nate head for Salway's, how's Miss Megan going to get home?"

"I'll ride Pirate, of course. I rode him over here. Now get going."

Megan could hear the booted foot of Charlie's lame leg scraping on the rocky ground as he hobbled away. "Come on, Nate," Charlie said, "we got work to do."

Nate did not reply, but she heard him fall in behind the old man. As the sound of their feet faded away, Megan spoke. "I'm sorry, Dan," she said, "about everything. Especially your paintings."

"I know."

"Why didn't you come to the Bar G last night if you had their horses?"

"There wasn't anything anybody could do. I needed some thinking time."

She noted the ragged edge in his voice now. "Did you save anything?"

"One painting. A portrait . . . Sol's. It was near the door. I intended to bring it over to the Bar G. It's yours."

"Mine?"

"Yes, it belongs in your home. At the Bar G . . . or wherever you're at."

"But I can't even see it."

"Not now. But maybe you will someday. The important thing is that you'll know it's there."

"But why?" she asked.

"I want you to have it."

"Then I accept it. Thank you," she said.

She was deeply moved by his gift, but somehow she felt he would be uncomfortable with an overt display of gratitude on her part. Then she felt a rough blistered hand close over hers, and she tensed and pulled her hand back reflexively before she relaxed and let him take it gently in his. He scooted away from the tree, and she felt his arm brush against her cotton shirt as he moved closer to her. He smelled of smoke and sweat, but she savored it for it was another way for her to know him—form an image of him—with her remaining senses. She did not speak, for she sensed somehow that all he wanted now was her nearness and her touch. And that she would gladly give him.

Nearly a half hour passed by her estimate before he spoke. "I owe you a horse," he said.

"What?"

"The mare. The strawberry roan. I had to shoot her. She was wounded in the gunfight. You can have the horse I left at your place in trade, if you like. I don't have a horse left here; they all died in the fire. For that matter, outside of raw land, everything I own is on me. Not much to show for thirty-two years, is it?"

"Some people never have that much. Besides, you've got talent . . . your mind. You can rebuild the house; stay at the Bar G till you do. Then you can paint again. There's got to be a market for work like yours."

"I thought you weren't so sure about my work," Dan said.

"I am now. I'll help you sell it if you like."

"I'd like that. I hate business details."

"Dan, do you know what would really gall old Dunkirk?"

"What's that?"

"If you start rebuilding your house right away. There hasn't been a place rebuilt yet that they've destroyed. It would be a way of letting them know that they're finished getting their way by violence. It would be like slapping the old man's face with a glove." She paused. "You aren't giving up, are you? You are going to stay?" She had tossed him a challenge. If she knew Dan McClure, he would pick it up.

"Well, I hadn't thought about it one way or another, but the idea of leaving hadn't even crossed my mind. I always had planned to replace the house; I need a studio with proper lighting."

"And you need a gallery to display your work. If people come here to buy your paintings, you can't have them strung out all over the floor. You don't want people tromping through your studio."

"Well, I doubt if anyone will come clear out in the Pine Ridge to buy my work. I'll have to take my paintings to a showing in Omaha, St. Louis, maybe back East at first. In a few years, the railroad will be going through Medicine Hill; people will be able to get here easier then."

"By that time, you'll have a reputation. We'll make them come here to buy your paintings."

"We?"

She hesitated. "Well, you said you wanted me to handle the sale of your paintings, didn't you?"

"Yes, that's right, I did."

"You're an artist and an engineer. You should be able to plan a beautiful home. Something that fits in the Pine Ridge. Not like that monstrosity of Dunkirk's."

"You don't like it either."

"Of course not."

"I do have some ideas," Dan said, "but I don't have the money to put them into action."

"You said your section's free and clear, and you've got your half interest in the land that Sol left us. You could borrow the money. Not in Medicine Hill, maybe, but in Ogallala. Dad did most of his banking in Ogallala because Dunkirk controlled the bank here. Your ranch would retire most of the debt, and you wouldn't have to borrow that much anyway. Think about it. The lumber's right here on your ranch, and there's a small sawmill a few miles west of Medicine Hill. We've got pockets of granite and limestone on Sol's land for stone if you want it."

"And labor?"

"How do you think most of the homes and buildings got built out here? Barn raisings, that's how. When you're ready to go, the neighbors will swarm in here like bees after clover. If you don't waste any time, you could have your new house and a barn, too, by winter."

"You make it sound so damned easy."

"It is. Try it. I dare you. You'll see."

He released her hand, and she felt his fingers gently touch her cheek as he turned her face toward his and tilted her chin upward. She knew that he was going to kiss her, just as she knew she would not resist. And when his lips touched hers, her own hand went to his cheek, caressing the stubble there for just a moment before he pulled his head away. His kiss had been soft, almost polite, but it had left her weak and warm, kindling a passion she had never felt before.

Dan seemed to retreat within himself again as they sat there silently. Was he sorry he had kissed her? Should she speak? Had she already said too much?

Finally Dan spoke. "I'll have to ride out and talk to Cal and the other ranchers tomorrow. And I've got a new house to plan. But before I take that on—"

"You're coming back with me to the Bar G for now," Megan said. "You need some rest. You can catch some sleep in Dad's old room . . . it gets the south breeze . . . after you eat some breakfast. And Dan—"

"Yes, what is it?"

"You sounded like a jackass when you were mumbling about paying for the dead roan."

"What? Oh yeah, I guess I did. But speaking of horses, your pinto's the only transportation we've got."

"She can carry us both if we go slow . . . and if you don't mind riding double," Megan said.

"I'll try to endure it."

Chapter 23

DAN SAT ASTRIDE the coyote dun stallion hidden in the dark shadows of the pine that rimmed the clearing. Here he was to rendezvous with the men who had been hand-picked by the Association's captains to ride with him on his mission to the Diamond D. He had asked for fifteen men, top hands who could handle their guns as well as ride. The guns were insurance; they wouldn't need them tonight if all went as planned.

The stallion snorted and tossed his head nervously, and Dan felt the horse tense beneath him. The dun's ears perked forward and Dan knew someone or something was working up the valley toward the clearing. Megan had insisted he take the stallion, a spirited, strong-willed animal that had run wild with a Wyoming herd before its capture. The Bar G had been unable to break the horse to the discipline and trustworthiness required of a cow pony, but it had not objected to stud service and according to Megan, had sired several crops of rangy, thickly muscled colts that were the talk of the Pine Ridge. The big animal was neither dwarfed nor intimidated by Dan's size and in spite of the animal's contrary ways, as Megan had predicted, Dan had taken an instant liking to the horse. Maybe it was because they were so much alike, he mused. Independent, freedom-loving, lusty.

"Take it easy, Atlas," Dan whispered as the horse reared slightly and danced uneasily. "Easy, boy."

It was Megan, she had confided, who had named the stallion for the titan of Greek mythology, but only Ben Grant, her learned teacher, understood the significance of the name. The hands just called the horse "the big stud."

Atlas's senses had not betrayed him. Dan could hear the soft thump of hooves against the ground, the crackling of dry twigs and underbrush, and the hushed voices of riders winding their way through the dense ponderosa. They moved cautiously into the clearing; some rode alone and others came in pairs. And as they caught sight of Dan, they reined in their horses and stood there waiting and watching, silently, their faces glowing in the moonlight like ghost riders in the night. Dan scrutinized the riders while they waited for the others to arrive. It was an eerie scene, somehow, the strange effect produced by the gray shadows that wavered with the breeze in the shimmering, silvery light cast by the moon which was half-hidden by a feather cloud cover.

Ghost riders. Dan tried to fix the image in his mind, attempted to breathe in the mood before he lost it. He had the title, the characters and the scene, and the colors . . . if he could hold them until he had a chance to paint them. He planted the picture in his mind with the thought he would resurrect it later.

Finally a single rider emerged from the trees. Unlike the others who sat slouched in their saddles, he rode erect and cocky. He passed through the other riders without so much as a pause and headed for Dan. He knew it was Tom Powell before he saw the man's face.

"Good evening, Tom," Dan said amicably.

"McClure."

He had not won Powell over, but if the man could keep a cool head, Dan had a hunch he would be handy to have around in a gun battle, or any other kind of fight, for that matter.

"Is everybody here?" Dan asked.

"I don't see anybody from Salway's bunch," Powell answered.

Ron Schwab

"They're covering the signal hills," Dan said. "And Cal's supposed to have two patrols out just in case there's trouble down the valley."

"What in the hell's this all about anyhow? I'll be damned if I like being kept in the dark about things. It makes a man feel like he's not trusted."

"We're going to pay a call on the Diamond D tonight."

"Does that mean what I think it means?"

"Probably not," Dan said as he nudged his stallion past Powell and moved across the clearing to where the other cowhands had been watching him and Powell curiously. Tom Powell fell in behind. "We've got work cut out for us tonight, men," Dan said as he rode in close. "I want to pay a call on the Dunkirk mansion." The cowboys looked at each other quizzically.

"You mean we're going to burn them out?" one man asked.

"No, we're going to let them know we can burn them out. I want to go on the Dunkirk place, get past their sentries, and deliver a personal message that the Diamond D is safe only as long as we're willing to let it be. So far, the damage has been inflicted on his neighbors. Maybe when Dunkirk sees it can work two ways, he'll look at things differently."

"If we're going to risk our balls riding in there," Powell growled, "then we'd just as well do some real damage. Burn the place down, maybe string up a few no-goods."

Dan heard a rumble of assent from the riders. "Your suggestion involves murder," Dan said. "Burning down the place would be just as wrong. Either way, we'd be breaking the law."

"That doesn't seem to bother Dunkirk none," Powell said. "And what law are you talking about? The only law around here is Dunkirk's. I say it's time we make some laws of our own."

"I'm not saying that it won't come to violence," Dan said, "but if it does, our small ranches will be burned out, too. More men will be killed. Maybe women and children."

"It's coming to that sooner or later anyhow," Powell countered.

"Maybe not. If we can show them tonight that the ranchers are organized and united, Dunkirk might give this another thought. If nothing else, maybe we'll learn something."

"Such as what?"

Dan ignored the question and turned to the other men. "When we formed the Association, it was agreed I'd call the shots. Any man who isn't willing to ride to the

Diamond D with that understanding can ride out now. I don't want you with me if you can't take orders."

All eyes focused on Dan, but no one rode away from the group. "Good," Dan said. "Now, we're going to split up into two groups. Half of you will come with me right down the road and through the main gate. The other half will go with Tom Powell."

Chapter 24

A BALL OF FIRE exploded in the meadow west of the Dunkirk ranch buildings and then another to the east. It was the signal that Tom Powell had cut through the barbed wire and worked his way to the vicinity of the Dunkirk house. And they had done it without firing a shot.

"Let's ride," Dan called to the fidgety riders who waited in a grove of swaying aspen just off the road. He reined the stallion onto the dirt road, and the others fell in behind as they headed towards the Diamond D at an even, unhurried gallop.

As they approached the gate, the two Dunkirk riders whose eyes had been fixed on the commotion near the ranch house swung their attention back to the road and the riders who bore down on them. One raised his Winchester to fire, when Dan called out, "Don't be a fool.

You're outnumbered. Open the gate and get out of the way." The second cowhand moved for the gate; the other shrugged, lowered his rifle and edged his horse off the road. Dan tipped his low-brimmed hat as they rode through the open gate and moved down the road toward the house. He glanced back over his shoulder and saw that the two sentries were staying put, apparently dumbfounded, as they watched the unexpected visitors file past.

One of the Tumbling T riders, a stocky, seasoned cowboy, pulled even with Dan. "How'd you know they wouldn't blow your head off?" he asked.

"I didn't," Dan said. "But an Army colonel told me once you can win seventy-five percent of your fights by sheer gall. Just scare the hell out of your enemy, and you can win a lot of your battles without lifting a gun. They call it psychology. It's a whole new science developing in Europe and the East. Think about it. Put yourself where those men were. There's some kind of ruckus being raised at the ranch house, then suddenly a bunch of gun slinging riders come charging down the road brazen as hell. Unless you're looking to be a martyr, you're going to think twice about gunplay. A hired gun or cowboy isn't going to be all that anxious to take a bullet."

"Yeah, that sure enough makes sense. That colonel of yours sounds like a smart man."

"His name was Custer."

"What? Well, I'll be damned."

"Fan out when we reach the ranch yard," Dan called to the men. "Stay in the shadows if you can." As they galloped into the yard, Dan caught sight of Tom Powell mounted on his black gelding near one corner of the front veranda of the house.

"You took long enough," Powell said as Dan separated from the other riders and moved toward Powell.

"You didn't leave anything for us to do," Dan said.

Powell smiled smugly. He was pleased with himself, and he should be. He had done a good job.

"We've got both doors of the bunkhouse covered," Powell said. "Anybody steps out, they'll get a gut full of lead. They'll stay put unless we push it."

"No reason for us to," Dan said. "We just want to keep them caged for a spell. Anybody hurt?"

"Not on our side. Couple of the Diamond D night riders are gonna have headaches for a few days, but they'll come around. They never knew what hit them. One thing troubles me, though."

"What's that?"

"Well, I knew we could do it, but it was too easy. By rights, with things being the way they have been, I would have looked for Dunkirk to have a few more men riding watch. We only came across two."

"There were only two at the gate," Dan said.

"Well, there didn't seem to be that many in the bunk-house, either. I suppose this time of year, the old man's got his hands spread out to his other places."

Dan nodded toward the house. "Any activity in there?"

"Nope. Dark as a cave. But you can bet they're awake; they're just waiting. I wouldn't try walking to the front door if I was you."

"I hadn't planned on it. I'll see if I can draw somebody out. Keep an eye on things, will you, Tom?"

"Yeah, Dan, you bet I will."

Tom Powell had just welcomed him to the Pine Ridge.

Dan dismounted and, dodging from one of the mammoth pillars to the other, maneuvered to the front of the house. "Sutherly," he called. "Are you in there?" There was no answer. "It's McClure. I want to talk."

One of the oak doors creaked open and Clay Sutherly, his hair disheveled, his shirt open to the waist, stepped out onto the veranda. His jaw was set firm, but otherwise, his face was passive and his eyes betrayed no fear.

He was unarmed. A man did not have to like Clay Sutherly to respect his courage and good sense.

Dan stepped out from behind the column that half hid him and moved slowly toward Sutherly. "It's after midnight," Sutherly said as they each stopped, not more than five feet apart, facing each other. "You picked a strange time to come visiting. I gather this isn't a social call."

"You guessed right," Dan said. "We stopped by to make an official announcement."

Sutherly's eyes swept the yard where the other ranchers and cowhands were scattered, watching silently and intently. "What kind of announcement?"

"About the formation of the Pine Ridge Cattlemen's Association."

"I've heard about it. Are you selling memberships?"

"Not to you, Sutherly. Not to the Diamond D. We came by to let you know that your days of burning and killing are over. After tonight we'll answer blow for blow, life for life."

"We don't take kindly to threats," Sutherly said.

"I'm not making threats. I'm making promises. We fired a few haystacks tonight; that's all. We're not going to do any more damage. I rode out here to show you that we have the support to fight a range war if that's what we've got to do, and the haystacks were burned to show you that we're capable of doing what we say."

"But you won't win anything."

"Everybody loses in this kind of fight," Dan said, "but this time the Diamond D is going to lose with the rest of us if you don't call off your dogs."

Sutherly met his gaze evenly. "You're making a mistake, McClure. A bad one. I've never ordered any harm done to the ranchers in this valley."

The man was telling the truth or he was a damned good liar. Probably the latter.

"Maybe. Maybe not. But if Dunkirk's ordered it, it's the same thing. See that he gets my message."

"Mr. Dunkirk hasn't, either. Let me tell you something, McClure. I'll admit we'd like to add to the Diamond D holdings. We want your place and the Bar G, but I'm not going to burn and kill for it. Neither would Mr. Dunkirk. He's too smart for that. He went through that in Texas. You're judging Mr. Dunkirk wrong . . . and me, too."

The man was some poker player. "Then who's responsible?" Dan asked.

"I wouldn't know."

Dan saw a flicker of uncertainty or nervousness in Sutherly's eyes.

"Dan, look to the south!"

It was Tom Powell's voice. Dan swung around and saw the orange-red glow of one of the signal fires on the ridge. "It's the Tyler section of the valley," Powell said.

"We'd better ride," Dan called. He turned back to Sutherly. "I hope you got the message. We don't want any more trouble."

"Like I told you, McClure, you're talking to the wrong man."

Dan whirled away and dashed for Megan's stallion.

Chapter 25

A S THE RIDERS raced their horses southeasterly towards the Tyler ranch, Dan caught a glimpse of what appeared to be a rider moving north-westerly across the ridge some distance off to his right. "Tom!" he yelled to Powell who rode a few paces behind. "Go on . . . I'll catch up later."

He reined Atlas to his right and peeled away from the others. Then he gave the powerful stallion free rein and spurred him ahead at breakneck speed as they angled across the moonlit range in the direction of the racing silhouette. He skirted the ridge rather than climb it, gambling that the rider was heading for the Diamond D, and, if so, would have to descend the rugged slope and cut across the meadow soon.

Moments later his gamble was proven justified as the horse barreled off a brush-sheltered trail and onto the meadow, not more than a hundred yards ahead of Dan and the stallion. "Let's take them, Atlas," Dan whispered, and as though understanding his rider's request, the stallion shot forward with a new burst of speed and began to close steadily on the other horse. The rhythm of the rider in front of him, the set in the saddle, was somehow familiar to Dan and then, as he drew closer, he knew why. The smaller horse was no match for the big stallion, and it had obviously been ridden hard this night, for its gait was halting and jerky now, its footing unsure, and as he bore in on the horse and rider, Dan could hear the animal's rasping gasps for wind.

"Liz," he yelled, "it's Dan. Pull up."

Liz Dunkirk looked back over her shoulder and slowed her horse, and as Dan drew even, finally reined in the wheezing, foot-sore animal. She threw her hat back over her head, brushing her hair through the strings that suspended it and tossed her head in that queenly, defiant way that was peculiarly hers.

She looked at Dan, her eyes challenging. "What are you doing out here this time of night?" he asked.

"None of your damned business," she said.

"I'm not so sure. There's apparently been trouble of some kind south of here. If you know anything about it, then what you're doing here is my business."

"Don't try to push me, mister. I'm not one of your vigilantes. I don't have to take orders from you."

"No, I suppose not. But if you know something, you could help a lot of people . . . including yourself. There won't be anything left of this valley . . . including the Diamond D . . . if we don't stop these raids. We delivered that message to your Mr. Sutherly tonight."

"Don't call him my Mr. Sutherly. I despise him. I hate him. I'll see him dead before the snow falls."

How had this raving, wild-eyed woman ever touched him so? Had he been that vulnerable, or had he, for a brief time, been given a glimpse of another side of Elizabeth Dunkirk?

She should have angered him by now, but he found himself more sad than angered. "I still want an answer," he persisted. "What are you doing out here at this hour? You nearly rode this horse to death."

"It's my horse. I'll do what I damn well please. As for the hour, if you must know, I often go riding at night. I like the . . . tranquility. When I have trouble sleeping, I go riding."

"Your horse doesn't look like it's been out for a quiet ride over the countryside." Her eyes were like frozen mountain lakes as she glared at him. "Where were you?"

"I said I don't have to answer your questions."

"Unless you have something to hide, there's no reason not to."

She hesitated before a beguiling smile began to spread on her face, but her eyes thawed only slightly. "It's embarrassing, but I wouldn't want you to get the wrong idea, Dan. We've been friends, such good friends. I have another friend, a gentleman, over on the east side of the valley. I've been meeting him occasionally ever since you . . . " her lips slipped into a feigned pout, "you cast me aside."

Dan ignored the bit of drama. "Why do you have to ride across the valley to meet him?"

"Would you come to my home? Make love to me in my bedroom?"

"No, of course not."

"My father and Sutherly hate this man. They'd kill him if he set foot on the place. Clay won't let any other man near me. He wants me for himself."

"Who's your rancher friend?"

"I won't tell. This is a private matter. You've asked me more than you have a right to the way it is, Dan. I've never told anyone about us, and I won't tell anyone about this man. I care very much for him."

"All right, let's say I believe your story. It still doesn't explain why you had to ride your poor horse into the ground."

"Clay doesn't know I leave the house. He'd beat the hell out of me if he found out." Her face scrunched up as though recalling unbearable pain. "He does terrible things to me. He's a cruel, sadistic man. I saw the fire on the ridge; I didn't know what it meant, but I knew somebody would see it, and it would wake up the ranch. And if Clay found out I wasn't in the house, I knew I'd be punished. I panicked and rode for home as fast as I could." She looked nervously in the direction of the Diamond D. "I've stayed here too long the way it is, Dan. I've got to go."

He sidled in closer to her now and took hold of her horses bridle. "Do you want me to ride back with you?"

"No, I'll be all right," she said.

"You'll have to go easy with this mare, or she'll never make it."

"I will. I promise. Thank you, Dan, for your concern."

"You know something, Liz?"

"What's that?"

"You're a damn poor liar. I don't believe a word you told me."

Her riding crop whipped out, lashing him solidly across his cheek and the bridge of his nose. He released his grip on the mare's bridle, but Liz slashed him again above the eye before he fended off a third blow with his forearm and grabbed her wrist and wrenched the crop from her hand. He flung the whip on the ground. "I think both your horse and I have had enough of that tonight."

"Bastard," she said, spitting out the words. "I hate you. I hate you."

"You seem to hate a lot of people. All of that hate's going to swallow you up if you don't watch out." She glared at him. "At least you confirmed it. I was right. You were lying to me. I've got a hunch if I can learn where you really were I'll unravel a lot of the answers about what's been happening in the Pine Ridge."

Suddenly, Liz dug her heels in the mare's flanks and the horse lunged forward. "Take it slow," Dan called after Liz Dunkirk as she rode away. "I'm not coming after you." He had nothing else to say to the woman, and the poor horse had earned a rest.

But Liz Dunkirk's appearance on the ridge had added a piece to the puzzle that seemed to be getting more complicated by the hour. Clay Sutherly's denial had been convincing and certainly the man had an alibi for anything that had happened this night. Of course, that didn't prove anything either way, for a man like Sutherly would be too clever to do his own dirty work. So there was still the possibility that others had been carrying on the raids under his orders.

But somehow Liz fit into this. He was almost certain of it. But he was less sure as to how and where.

He turned the stallion south and had an uneasy feeling he was headed on a journey to more carnage and smoke and ashes.

Chapter 26

DAN SAT ACROSS from Megan at the oak table in the Grant house. He had ridden in only a few hours earlier, bone weary and weak, and after giving Megan only a sketchy accounting of the previous night's events, he had drug himself into Ben Grant's old room, collapsed on the brass bed, and plummeted into a dead sleep. The redolent smell of fresh ham and hot-cakes had awakened him, though, and he found himself surprisingly rejuvenated and energetic now as he washed down the hearty breakfast with a cup of steaming java.

Most of the hands had eaten and left for their assigned chores before Dan made an appearance at the table. Charlie and Nate had departed shortly after. Nate had been quiet and moody, if not hostile, since Dan moved into the Grant house. Dan knew it rankled the young man that he was staying there, and although Megan seemed to be blithely unaware of Nate's unhappiness, Dan knew jealousy when he saw it. He sympathized with Nate Coates, but he was as helpless to wash away the youthful cowboy's longings as he was to deny his own growing feelings for Megan Grant.

"Dan," Megan asked, "should I send some men over to help at Chris Tyler's?"

"No, I don't think so. Not today. They'll need some help later to raise a new barn. The raiders didn't touch anything else."

"I'm just glad nobody was hurt or killed," Megan said.

"We can thank the Association for that. Chris said they couldn't have kept the gunmen at bay much longer. Two of their cowhands were with me at Dunkirk's, so it was just the Tylers and one hand against seven or eight raiders. He said when the signal fire went up on the ridge, they lost their stomach for a fight because they didn't stick around long after that. It could have been a lot worse."

"He didn't recognize any of the raiders?"

"No, they were masked. He said there were two other riders on the rise west of the house who must have been their leaders."

"Why did he say that?"

"Well, he said one of the raiders rode out to them and seemed to get some instructions before he came back and called to the others to ride off."

"Well, at least you know Clay Sutherly wasn't there," Megan said.

"Yes, but I don't think that necessarily clears him."

"Do you think Liz Dunkirk was one of the two?"

He looked over at Megan. It was hard to believe she was blind. Her clear green eyes were alive and alert with a light he had never seen in a blind person before. He would go mad if he didn't have a chance to paint that face soon. When he went into Medicine Hill later, he would see about telegraphing Omaha for some supplies. His old friend, Frank Riley, would know what he needed. Maybe Frank could ship them by train to Ogallala, and Dan could intercept the merchandise there.

"Dan, you didn't answer me. Do you think Liz Dunkirk was there?"

"I don't know yet." He hesitated. "Yes. Yes, I think she was."

"You sound so strange whenever I mention Liz Dunkirk. Were you in love with her?"

"No, I liked her. I . . . I found her attractive."

"I'm sure you did. Most men do . . . so I hear."

Dan changed the subject. "I'm going to ride into Medicine Hill. If you want me to pick you up anything in town, let me know before I leave. I thought I'd see how Mr. Battie is coming along on settling the estate, maybe have another chat with the sheriff."

"The sheriff? Why?"

"He's the official representative of the law around here. I want to keep him informed about the activities of the Cattlemen's Association. I wouldn't want him to get the wrong impression."

He saw the muscles in her fine jaw and neck tense and read the apprehension in her face. "It's more than that, Dan. I don't know what it is, but you have another reason. Tell me. Please don't keep things from me."

He reached over and took her hand in his. "I'm not trying to keep things from you, Megan. I honestly don't have anything special in mind. I just think I should talk with Keaton. We know he's close to the Diamond D, and we aren't getting answers anywhere else. There's just a chance he'll let something slip."

"I'm afraid of him. He's like a cat. He likes to play with his victim, and he'd kill just for the pleasure of killing. I know he would."

"Well, you might be right. But I don't intend to be one of his victims."

"Others have probably said that," she said softly. She withdrew her hand from his. "But you'll do what you have to do, won't you?"

"Yes, I will."

Chapter 27

LUCAS BATTIE, WHILE still a bit stuffy, was more relaxed and less formal than he had been at their first meeting, the day he read Sol's will. Dan found legal and business matters boring, but as near as he could tell, Battie had been handling Sol's estate matters fairly and efficiently. There was a shrewd mind behind the cherubic, innocent-looking face.

He sat in Battie's office now, reviewing the paperwork that Battie had completed since their last session. "We should have this cleared up within the next two months," Battie said. "There have been no claims filed against Mr. Pyle's estate, so I can now petition the county court for a final decree. It's very routine. The judge will sign an order transferring the land in undivided interests to you and Miss Grant. The personal property, the cattle and so forth, will be assigned to Miss Grant alone. I'm afraid my fees and other costs will take the small amount of cash Mr. Pyle had, but you shouldn't be forced to liquidate anything."

"I'm glad for that," Dan said. "I'm well satisfied, Mr. Battie, but I am curious about something. Maybe you could enlighten me."

"I will if I am able."

"Why did Sol leave me the interest in the land? I've never understood it. I only knew him a few months."

"He never discussed it with you?"

"He told me he'd made a will, and it was in your office. That's all."

"I see. Well, I don't recollect precisely what Mr. Pyle said at the time we made out his will, but I can relate the gist of it. He trusted you implicitly, I can assure you of that. He said he had an instinct about men that had never led him astray. If you don't mind my saying so, he thought you were rather strange. He could not quite fathom why a man would devote his life to 'painting pictures' as he called it, and he thought it was something of a waste."

"Yes," Dan said, "I know Sol never quite understood my artistic pursuits. But he seemed to accept it and didn't hold it against me too much. He even sat for a portrait."

"Yes, he mentioned that, and I think, deep down, he was quite proud of it. Anyway, he said you were one of those rare men he had encountered who was true to himself, and he had an expression . . . what was it? Cowboy talk has always intrigued me, and I try to catalog these things in my mind. Oh, yes, he said your word was as binding as a hangman's knot. Yes, that's what it was. Interesting, isn't it? I should think you would take it as a compliment."

"Yes, I do. I don't know that he was right, but it's something to live up to. But that's no reason to leave me a half interest in his ranch."

"I suppose not." Battie furrowed his brow and rubbed his temple thoughtfully. "Something else, as I recall, something that made little sense at the time and still defies understanding, unless—"

"Unless what?"

"You and Miss Grant," Battie said. "You're not betrothed, are you?"

"No, hardly. And at the time Sol made his will, Meg and I were barely speaking."

"I see."

"What did he say?" Dan asked.

"Well, I'm almost certain he said that sooner or later the ranch would get put back together anyway."

Dan shook his head in disbelief. Had the old buzzard been matchmaking from the grave? Certainly, his death and the common ownership of the land had pushed him and Megan toward friendship again, and now they were more than friends. But he didn't know yet how much more. He could just see old Sol sitting on a cloud somewhere grinning at his small joke.

Dan pushed his chair back from Battie's desk. "Thank you, Mr. Battie. You've been very helpful."

"I hope so, Mr. McClure. If there's anything else, please don't hesitate to get in touch with me."

Dan started to rise but then sat back down. "There is something else."

"Yes?"

"Do you represent Mr. Dunkirk or his enterprises?"

"No, sir. Woodson Dunkirk and I never quite saw eye to eye. He obtains his legal counsel in Ogallala, I believe. He also retains an Omaha firm for some of his more complex dealings.

"Good. Then perhaps we can speak freely about Mr. Dunkirk."

"I should think so."

"Do you think Dunkirk's the kind of man to order the attacks that have been taking place on the small ranchers?"

"I doubt it. Not if he was in his right mind."

"Why not?"

"Ten years ago, perhaps even five, one could understand a greedy, lawless man seeking such an approach. Understand it, mind you, but not approve it. But we have a sound system of law developing in this state. The criminal law is still lax in the Panhandle, but it's coming, and an intelligent man like Mr. Dunkirk would see that. I don't think he would risk his empire in such blatant ways. It troubles me to say this, but I suspect he would employ lawmakers to accomplish his objectives by more legitimate methods. And I never felt that Mr. Dunkirk was a violent man. I have been here some years, and there was never anything in his nature to indicate it. There was no violence until about two years ago. No, I do not necessarily accept the popular assumption that Mr. Dunkirk is behind the raids."

"What about his foreman, Clay Sutherly?"

"I can't say. I've seen the man on the street occasionally, but I've never met him. Folks tell me that the man is intensely loyal to Woodson Dunkirk and that he seems to be in love with Mr. Dunkirk's daughter. It was evidently reciprocated at one time, I am told, but they have had a falling out in recent months. She's quite headstrong, I gather, and there seems to be some dispute over who will eventually control the ranch. There's a great deal of speculation over what will become of it. Mr. Dunkirk has apparently anointed Mr. Sutherly as his successor to the throne, and it would be only natural, I suppose, that he would find Mr. Sutherly's marriage to his daughter very gratifying. I always wondered if Miss Dunkirk's friendship with the other gentleman was the destructive influence on her relationship with Mr. Sutherly."

"Are you talking about her rancher friend?"

"I know nothing about a rancher. I was referring to her friendship with Sheriff Keaton."

"Liz Dunkirk and Keaton? They're friends?"

"It would seem so. I hope it doesn't appear unseemly of me, but I have a clear view of the sheriff's office from my window. I've seen Miss Dunkirk enter his office on many occasions the past several years, as often as two or three times a week. They're never seen together socially, but she has been in his office sometimes for as long as several hours. Of course, I'm not one to gossip, and I feel a bit uncomfortable relating this."

Dan stood and extended his hand to the portly lawyer. "Mr. Battie, you've been very helpful. I can't thank you enough."

The lawyer rose and accepted Dan's hand. "I'm afraid I don't understand."

"I have to be going now, Mr. Battie. I'll explain some other time. Thanks again."

Chapter 28

AFTER LEAVING LAWYER Battie's office, Dan strolled over to the telegraph office and dispatched a message to Omaha for art supplies. He informed the telegrapher that he would return in a few days to see if there was any response.

As he stepped out onto the boardwalk, he debated whether to pay a call on Sheriff Stiles Keaton. His only motive was to badger and needle, hoping that Keaton would make some slip that would unlock the door to a lot of answers he was looking for. But it was a little like teasing a rattlesnake, he decided. You could tease it for a long time without getting bit, but if you moved too slowly just once, you could end up dead.

No, he decided, it was not time to face Keaton. There were still a few things he wanted to know before he confronted the man.

As he walked back up the street in the direction of the lawyer's office where he had hitched the stallion, Dan saw that the decision had been made for him. Keaton, with his butt resting on the hitching rail, stood next to the horse and sucked contemplatively on a cigar. The sheriff looked up when he heard Dan approaching, but his reptilian eyes did not so much as blink to acknowledge Dan's presence.

The sheriff turned slowly away, fixing his eyes on some invisible object across the street and blew out a billowing, perfect ring of smoke. Dan strolled slowly toward the sheriff who blocked his path to the stallion.

"You looking for me, Sheriff?" he asked.

"Not necessarily."

"Fine, then I'll be on my way."

Keaton stood up and brushed some imaginary dust off his black trousers before he spoke. "But as long as you're here, I thought we might have a few words."

"If you like. What can I do for you?"

"I've been hearing some rumors about some vigilante activity in the hills. A cattlemen's organization."

"There is a new organization, yes. The Pine Ridge Cattlemen's Association. I'm acting as temporary president."

"Then I'm talking to the right man. McClure, I won't have people taking the law into their own hands. I've heard about some things I don't like."

"Is that right? If you'll tell me about them, Sheriff, maybe I can clear up any gossip."

Despite his outward calm, Dan noticed that the sheriff's hands and neck were tense, like flattened wire coils ready to spring.

"I've been told," Keaton said, "that this association of yours is stirring up trouble. Making threats on the Diamond D. I got word this morning that you and some other men raided the Dunkirk place last night, set some fires, injured some men. I'll be riding out there this morning to talk to Mr. Dunkirk and his people. If what I heard is true, I'll be making some arrests."

"For what?" Dan asked.

"Trespass. Assault. No doubt some other laws were broken too."

"Is that what you're here for? To arrest me? If so, I'm unarmed. I'll go peacefully."

"No. Not yet. I'm just giving you fair warning. Let me take care of any problems in this county. If your Association keeps sending out patrols, somebody's going to get hurt before long."

"We've already been hurt, Sheriff, and we haven't seen any sign that you've done anything about it. That's why we organized the Association. We'd like nothing better than to get back to our own business interests, but you don't seem to care much about what's going on unless it works for Dunkirk."

"Are you accusing me?"

Dan chose not to reply directly to the sheriff's query. "While you're out at Dunkirk's place, Sheriff, you might swing by the Tumbling T. Chris Tyler had his barn burned to the ground last night, and we've got good reason to believe he and his family wouldn't be alive today if it weren't for the Cattlemen's Association."

"Oh? This is the first I've heard of it."

The sheriff sounded bored. Was this the time to probe for an answer? He would never have a better opportunity; he was sure of that.

"There's one thing I don't understand, Sheriff."

Keaton's eyes narrowed. "What's that?"

"I don't see how you and Miss Dunkirk missed all the hell that was raised in the hills last night."

The sheriff's face flashed white, and Dan caught the fleeting moment of panic in his eyes. Keaton had been with Liz last night.

"Who says I was with Miss Dunkirk last night?"

The sheriff was moving cautiously, not denying it, but testing to see just how much Dan knew. Well, he would let the lawman think he knew a lot more than he did. "Several of our men said they saw you and Miss Dunkirk near the Tyler place last night. They couldn't figure out why you didn't lend a hand. You know one of them even had the silly notion that you were in cahoots with the raiders. Ridiculous, isn't it?"

The sheriff flicked his half-smoked cigar on the street and ground it into the fine dust with his boot. "Your men were mistaken, or they lied."

"Well, I'd like to think so. But they were damned positive about what they saw. A man can't help but wonder," Dan said.

Keaton opened his mouth to speak, but then closed it, drawing his thin lips tight. He wheeled away from Dan and walked away, heading toward his office across the street with quick, deliberate steps.

So Keaton's involvement was more than passive. And Liz obviously knew more than Dan had ever suspected. But who was giving the orders? Dunkirk? Clay Sutherly?

Dan had a feeling that he had all the pieces to the puzzle now, if he could just put them together. He stepped over to Atlas and rubbed the big stallion's muzzle gently. The horse accepted the show of affection for a moment;

then, as if remembering some distant hurt, he tossed his head defiantly. "It's all right, boy," Dan said as he mounted. "I understand. It all takes time. Maybe we'll both find some peace soon."

Chapter 29

MEGAN LISTENED AS Dan's pencil traveled across the thick parchment paper. She tried to visualize the sketches that were unfolding there. She could not explain it, but for some reason not being able to see what he was doing now pained her more than anything had since the early days of her blindness. She sat beside him at the kitchen table. They spent most of their time together at this table, and she savored these moments as much as she loathed the hours he was away.

The Pine Ridge had been quiet now for the better part of two weeks, not that anyone thought the days of flame and bloodshed had passed. It was a lull. Dan had called it the calm before the storm. She knew it was more than intuition on his part; something had happened the day he rode into Medicine Hill. He had bottled it up inside him, trying to spare her anguish, she assumed. It didn't work that way. It only frightened her, leaving her with a sense of impending tragedy.

Dan's voice broke into her thoughts. "We finished clearing the site this afternoon. Cal's sending some men up to help lay the foundation the day after tomorrow."

"Do you have enough limestone?"

"Yeah. I think we've got enough for the fireplace and the foundation."

"I'm glad you're nestling the new house in closer to the hills. It will be cozier, don't you think?"

"Yes. We'll have better protection from the winds. I hadn't planned to build anything this large, but I'll be able to use all native materials, and I want this place to last a long time. I don't want to interrupt my work again with adding on."

"What are you sketching now?" she asked.

"I'm making some changes on the room arrangements."

"Why I thought we'd decided . . . you're not doing anything to the gallery, are you?"

"No, the studio and the gallery are just like we agreed on. There's a separate entrance to the gallery, so it will have access without interfering with the living quarters."

"So what are you changing?"

"Well, I hadn't said anything about it before, but I've added to the plans since we talked about them earlier."

"Did you decide to put on a second story?"

"No, I just added to one wing."

She was slightly hurt that he had not discussed it with her, but it was his house, she reminded herself. It was none of her concern. "What . . . what exactly are you doing?"

"I was thinking about it about a week ago," he said. "The home was everything an artist could want. Working space, atmosphere, display rooms. But I'm not going to paint 24 hours a day . . . at least not every day."

"I would think not."

"I've decided there wasn't enough room to live in," Dan said.

"You have to be joking. You have a parlor, a study, a kitchen."

"There's only one bedroom."

"Well, yes, but—"

"I decided to expand that bedroom and add two more."

"But why?" Megan asked.

"I don't want to live there alone. I don't think I even want to build it if I have to live there alone."

"I don't understand."

"I want to share my life with someone. I want a woman, and I want children. There's no better country for raising children, sons and daughters who will be strong and free and creative. It would be a crime against nature for me to hole up in a big house like that and paint my life away. Besides, after a time, I don't think I'd be much of an artist. You can't paint life without living it. I've thought about that. I know you can't. My best work came from what I lived."

"Including Angela?" Megan asked impishly.

"Damn it. Yes. Including Angela."

"I was just teasing."

"I know you were. I have a way of taking myself too seriously. Somehow this isn't coming out the way I'd planned it."

"You mean the house?"

"No, I don't mean the house. I'm referring to this speech."

"Oh, you're giving a speech. I'm glad you paint better than you speak, or there wouldn't be much hope for you."

Why was she fencing with him this way? Was she afraid of what he was going to say?

Megan heard Dan slide his chair back and get up from the table. Was he angry at her? Was he leaving? Damn, if she could just see his face, read what was in his eyes.

He took her hand. "Megan Grant, stand up and face me," he said, his voice severe.

She hesitated, confused and mystified, and then rose slowly. He released her hand and she felt his hands close gently on her shoulders, and as she faced him, her legs trembled, and she felt weak at his touch. Her heart raced frantically as she struggled to control the turbulent emotions that swept over her.

"Dan, I—"

"Don't say a word, Megan. Just this once. Let me say what I've got to say."

She was more than willing to hear him out, for his actions had addled her brain, dried her throat and left her tongue-tied.

"Meg, I knew it was building to this. It has been since we first met. But at first you seemed like such a child. I know different now. You're a woman, a sensitive, intelligent, strong woman."

"Dan, please—"

"Let me finish, Meg. I said I can't paint without living any more than I can live without painting. When I think of life and living, your face is always there. I can't separate my life from yours. Oh, hell, I can't be making any sense. Why don't I just say it . . . I'm in love with you, Meg. You're the one I want to share the rest of my life with. We planned the house together. We put both our hearts into that home. It's as much yours as it is mine, maybe more. I didn't change much. Just enough to make room for you and our children." His grip on her shoulder tightened and then relaxed. "I'm asking you to marry me, Meg."

Suddenly her eyes burned and she felt the tears stream down her cheeks as his lips touched her forehead. "Dan, I . . . I don't know what to say." Was that her squeaky, crackly voice that said that?

"You don't have to say much, Meg. Will you marry me? All I need is one word."

"No," she said, her voice shaky. "I'm sorry, Dan. I can't. No." Her body began to shake spasmodically. "I'm sorry."

She tore away from him, knocking over the chair, disoriented for a moment as she wandered helplessly about the room. She got her bearings and clumsily made her way out of the kitchen and rushed to the bedroom. Once inside, she closed the door, pushed the bolt that locked it, and threw herself on the bed, surrendering to the sobs that racked her body.

* * *

She had not remembered falling asleep, and the dull, persistent throbbing in her temple told her she had not slept all that long. The night chill had left her bedroom, and the tantalizing smell of frying bacon confirmed that it was well past sunrise and that someone else was tending to the kitchen chores. Why hadn't Charlie awakened her? She raised herself up and swung her legs off the bed, sitting there for a spell, trying to shake off the unfamiliar grogginess that numbed her brain. Only then did she realize that she was still in the gingham dress she had worn the night before.

Then she remembered: Dan's proposal. And she had said no to the man whose mere touch set her heart racing and made her knees weak. She had said no to the man whose voice chased away the fears of what she could not see, to the man whose nearness made her feel warm and serene. With Dan McClure she was bold, confident, unafraid of the future. Selfishly, she thought, Dan McClure could give her everything she wanted from life, and she loved him dearly. What she felt for Dan was the most unselfish emotion she had ever known. She wanted to give as well as take, be his lifeline as he was hers, supporting, sustaining and loving him through the years ahead.

But an artist married to a blind woman? A woman who could not even view the ultimate expression of his soul? A man like Dan, sensitive and imaginative, had to speak through his paints and oils. How could she hear him in the ways that meant so much to both of them if she could not see his work? It would break her heart someday to be cut off from that vital part of Dan McClure.

But did he understand? She wanted him to. It was important to her that he did. She had to explain. She got up and stood beside the bed for a moment, orienting herself before she moved to the door and made her way slowly to the kitchen. As she entered the kitchen, she could tell by the silence that the cowhands were gone. She could hear someone standing at the wood stove, stirring the bacon that crackled in the hot grease of the skillet. Biscuits were baking, too, and their aroma made her ravenous in spite of her melancholy.

"Good morning, Meg," came the cook's voice.

"Dan?"

"Of course. I thought I should make myself useful. I helped Charlie with breakfast. Sit down. There's just enough left for you."

"I am hungry," she said and moved toward the table.

Dan did not appear upset this morning. Perhaps he was relieved. It was possible that he had asked her to marry him out of some sense of obligation or pity, she thought.

Dan set a plate in front of her as she sat down. He stepped away and returned momentarily. She heard two distinct sounds as he placed something else on the table. One was china; that could be the coffee cup. The other was a dull thud she did not recognize.

"Coffee's to your right," Dan said. "Honey jar to the left. I thought you might like some with the biscuits."

He took a seat across the table from her, and as she ate silently, she knew he was watching her, studying her. She did not need eyes to tell her that.

Finally, when she was nearly finished, he spoke. "I'm going to ride over to my place this morning. There are a few things I have to finish up before they start the foundation work tomorrow."

"You're going ahead, then, the way you planned?"

"Yes, of course. Why not?"

"I . . . I don't know." She hesitated. "Dan, I'd like to explain . . . about last night."

"No, don't explain. Not now, anyway."

"But I want to. I'm afraid you don't understand."

"Why don't you ride along with me? We can talk on the way if you'd like."

"You want me to ride with you after last night?" Megan asked

"You're sure making a fuss over last night. Sure, I want you to ride with me. You've got to check out your property."

He kept talking in riddles. He was not making any sense at all. "What do you mean 'my property?'" she asked.

"One way or another, you're going to own that house. The whole ranch, for that matter. It's meant to be with the Bar G."

She heard him get up and walk to the window.

"I'm going to build that damned house, Megan Grant, just the way we planned it, come hell or high water. And I didn't hear anything you said last night, so you'd better be thinking about what your answer's going to be the next time I ask the same question. If it's yes, it's our house, our ranch. If it's no, it's your house, your ranch. Because, before I leave, I'm going to deed it over to you and let you have it as a monument to your stubbornness."

"That's the most ridiculous thing I ever heard of. What a stupid way to get revenge."

"Revenge? What do I have to get revenge for?"

"Well . . . well, because I said no. Because I said I wouldn't marry you."

"I didn't hear you say that," he said.

"Damn you, Dan, you're driving me crazy with this conversation. All right, if you didn't hear me the first time, I'll say it again so you can save the trouble and expense of building that fool house of yours."

"Ours," he corrected and started to move for the door. "And, if you want to tell me anything else, you'll have to say it on horseback. Do you want me to saddle your pinto?"

"No," she snapped. Then, as she heard him open the door, "Oh, go ahead," she called after him. "You can saddle my horse, but I have to go wash up and change into some riding clothes."

"Take your time," he said, "I'll bring the horses by the house."

Chapter 30

MEGAN STEPPED OUT onto the porch. Her mood was brightened by the change to boots and riding britches. She felt more herself in the doeskin shirt Sol had given her than in the cumbersome dresses and petticoats she had been wearing too much of lately. The morning breeze that drifted off the Pine Ridge caressed her face and refreshed her. Her mind was clear now even though the dull aching in her head persisted. She moved to the edge of the porch and waited till she heard the two horses approach. One was light-footed and quick of gait; the other's steps sounded heavier and slower, a larger animal with a longer stride.

"You're riding Atlas, aren't you?" Megan asked as Dan rode up to the front of the porch.

"Yes, I'm kind of partial to the ornery devil."

"A man your size needs a big horse," she said, stepping cautiously off the porch.

Suddenly, several quick, knifelike pains sliced through her temples, and she flinched against the white glare that exploded momentarily in her head. She stumbled but regained her balance as her hands found the neck of the pinto Dan had edged in front of her.

"Meg? What is it? Are you all right?"

She barely heard Dan's voice through the ringing in her ears. "I'm fine," she lied. "I just tripped when I came off the steps." The pain subsided now, and the fog in her head ebbed away. Her hands grasped the saddle horn, and she worked her foot into the stirrup before she lifted herself on an uncertain, trembling leg into the saddle.

"Meg, you look like you've seen a ghost," Dan said. "Are you sure you're all right?"

"Yes, I'm fine." A ghost. It could have been, she thought; it was white. The overpowering sense of whiteness, for just a few moments, had displaced the endless blackness she had known since the night she lost her sight.

It was Megan who broke the silence this time as their horses moved off the slope and out onto the meadow on Dan's side of the ridge that separated his place from the Bar G. Slowing the pinto to a walk, she said, "You said I could explain about last night."

"And I also told you I didn't hear what you said."

"And you say I'm stubborn," she countered.

"I'm not stubborn; I'm persistent."

"I don't see the difference."

"It might be perspective," he conceded. "But Meg, I would have accepted your answer if I believed you meant it. I care for you too much to press you into something you don't want. Let me approach it differently . . . I asked you if you would marry me. You said no. Do you care for me, Meg?"

"Of course I do."

"Do you love me?"

"You're cornering me."

"Yes, I suppose so. Do you?" She did not answer. "Megan, do you love me?"

"Yes." Then she added quickly, "But that doesn't mean I'll marry you."

"Oh, yes it does. That's why I haven't walked away. Because you are going to be my wife, Megan Grant. And I'm going to be your husband, and we're going to live in our house. Now explain that away . . . and don't throw me some horse dung about your blindness being a burden. Martyrdom doesn't become you."

"I'm not trying to be a martyr, Dan. It has to do with your paintings."

"My paintings?"

"I couldn't marry you, spend a lifetime with you, without being able to see your work. It would kill me not being able to share that part of you. I'd never know you the way I want to know you if I couldn't see your paintings. Day by day, month by month, it would tear me to pieces."

"But I'll tell you about my paintings," he said. "I'll describe them to you. I'll explain what I was thinking when I did them. You can ask me questions. I won't deny you any part of me, I promise. You're making too much of your blindness. I need you, Meg, more than you need me, I'm afraid. I don't know if I can paint without you. There truly is something called artistic inspiration; it's a thing you can't put your finger on, but it's there."

"Dan, you were painting before you met me. You'll paint again no matter what happens."

"All right, maybe I was exaggerating somewhat; perhaps I would paint. But with you I can be the kind of artist that I can't be without you, because I need the kind of emotions you bring out in me to paint what I want to paint. If a writer wants to write about love, he has to know love and feel love. So does an artist who wants to paint love."

He was overpowering her with his words, and she was hard pressed to think of a comeback. She wanted to believe what he said, but she didn't trust her judgment right now.

"You sound like a character in a romantic novel," she said.

"I suppose I do," he admitted. "I am a romantic."

"We all are in some ways," she said.

"Yes, but I'm too much of one. I spend too much time lost in dreams. That's another reason I need you. Remember? You said you would market my work and look after the business side of my work. You can't do that very well if you're living at the Bar G. Megan, we planned the house together. Don't tell me you never saw yourself in it."

She did not reply for she could not deny it without lying, and she would not lie again to him. Never.

"Meg," he said, "I want to put Sol's portrait on one wall of the parlor. I want to put yours on the opposite wall."

"Mine?"

"Yes, I want to paint yours next. Don't you think Sol would like that? The two of you looking across the room at each other?"

"Yes. Yes, I think he would."

"But Sol's painting has to hang in your house, Meg, and your painting has to hang in mine, so it looks like you'll have to marry me. It's an awful dilemma."

"I wish I could see Sol's portrait," she said wistfully.

"Maybe you will someday. Don't give up hope. But in the meantime, let me be your eyes."

She opened her mouth to speak and the whiteness, bright and glaring, flashed across her eyes and struck her dumb. Then it wasn't white anymore; it was gold and orange and red. Flaming crimson. Colors. Not blackness. Not whiteness. Distinctive, vivid colors. The sun?

"Meg, you've got that look again. Are you sure you're all right?"

"I . . . I don't know. I feel strange . . . a little dizzy."

"We'll be home in a few minutes. I'll get you under some shade. Maybe it's the heat; the sun's terribly bright this morning."

"Yes, it is," she said. "I mean, it's very hot."

As they rode up the wagon trail that led to the charred remains of Dan's ranch building, Megan was awestruck at the kaleidoscope of colors that was unfolding before her. Greens and blues and browns and fuzzy blotches of colors. But colors, just the same. Was it possible? She dared not raise her hopes. She could not tell Dan. Not yet. It might break the spell and wash away this beautiful dream.

As the horses trotted into the ranch yard, Dan edged the stallion in front of the pinto and led them to a screen of ponderosa. Megan knew they were ponderosa because she caught the fresh scent of pine and felt the cooling shade of their boughs. But what struck her most was the dark curtain of green that spread before her. They dismounted there, and Dan tethered the horses to a low tree limb nearby.

"How are you feeling now?" he asked.

"Better. I'm still a little dizzy, though."

He took her arm and led her to the base of the towering tree. She knew because she could make out the blurry outline of its trunk.

"Why don't you sit here for a spell?" he said. "I forgot to fill my canteen before I left, but I'll get some fresh water from the well."

Megan's eyes tracked the gray image of Dan McClure as he stepped over to the stallion and retrieved the canteen that was hitched to his saddle and then headed across the ranch yard. He was the Dan McClure she remembered: tall, strong, purposeful in the long strides of his walk.

Dan filled his canteen with cold well water at the pump. He straightened up and looked back at Megan who sat Indian style in the shade some fifty yards away. She was acting strangely, he thought, casting her head about like a young doe about to venture out onto a meadow. Her attention seemed to focus on one thing and then would suddenly dart to another. At least she appeared alert now; earlier she had seemed groggy and confused and several times had flinched noticeably as though suffering some sort of pain. Something was bothering her, but she had been evasive and had denied him any clue as to what was ailing her.

He flung the canteen over his shoulder and took a few steps in Megan's direction, but stopped when he saw the two riders galloping up the road toward the ranch yard. He recognized Liz Dunkirk's golden flowing mane on one of the riders. The tall, black-garbed man was Stiles Keaton.

Dan moved to meet the approaching riders. It would be interesting to see what this pair had to say.

As they pulled up in front of him, Dan noted the two were grim-faced, and he saw something akin to fear in Liz Dunkirk's eyes that made him wary. The sheriff's eyes betrayed nothing but smoldering contempt.

"We've been watching for you, McClure," Keaton said. "I think it's time we talked again."

"I've said all I have to say," Dan replied. "But it looks like I was right. You and Liz were there when the Tylers were raided. And I suppose the others, too? I'm curious, Keaton. Who killed Ben Grant and Sol Pyle? Was it you, or do you just kill women?" Dan's hand inched toward his revolver.

Keaton's own six-gun spun into his hand, seemingly from nowhere and was leveled at Dan's chest before he even touched the butt of his own gun. The lean man was as quick as he looked. Lightning quick.

"Unbuckle your gun belt, McClure, and let it drop, or you're a dead man."

Keaton had the drop on him. It would be suicide not to obey. But the odds were not good either way. He unfastened his belt buckle and the gun belt, and the holstered pistol thudded into the dust at his feet. He could not believe it. Keaton wasn't taking any chances. He intended to kill him in cold blood; he would have to kill Megan, too. All Dan could do was to buy time and hope that someone came along. Or that something happened to give him a chance.

"You didn't answer my questions about the killings," Dan said.

"You're not in a position to ask questions, but I guess I can grant a dying man his last wish," Keaton said. "I did in Sol Pyle myself. Our hired guns took care of the others."

"And you and Liz have been behind the raids?"

"More or less."

"Where does Clay Sutherly fit in?"

"He doesn't fit in at all. He's next . . . after you and your bitch. After he's out of the way, Miss Dunkirk will petition the court for her appointment as her father's guardian."

"And you'll more or less take Sutherly's place, I presume?"

"More or less. Likely more."

Dan looked up at Elizabeth Dunkirk. "Why, Liz? Why the lies? Why the charade? The killings? None of it makes sense."

Her face was pale as death; her eyes wild and frantic like a cornered jack rabbit.

"The killings weren't my idea. I only wanted Sutherly dead. I thought he would be blamed for the raids and then my father would get rid of him . . . or someone else would kill him."

"Like me?"

"Yes."

"If you were hiring gunfighters, why didn't you just hire someone to kill Sutherly?"

"Because we needed the land to expand the ranch, too. I thought we could make it all work together."

"Kill two or three birds with one stone, so to speak. Is that it?" Dan asked.

"I didn't want it to come to this, Dan." She glanced nervously at Keaton. "I still don't. I begged him not to come here. I don't want you dead, Dan."

"Then call off the dog."

"I . . . I can't."

"You mean you won't."

"She means she can't," Keaton said. "She's in too deep. She's my property now; she'll be my woman as soon as we get control of the ranch."

"You're a fool, Liz," Dan said. "You'd have been better off to throw your lot in with Sutherly than to take up with this piece of human garbage. A murderer who hides behind a tin star."

The hammer of Keaton's pistol clicked back. "You've said your piece, mister."

"No, Stiles, no!" Elizabeth Dunkirk screamed, yanking on the reins of her horse and driving it into Keaton's. The sheriff's horse lurched forward crashing its shoulder against Dan and catapulting him backwards onto the crusty earth. Keaton's gun whipped out and the barrel slammed into Liz Dunkirk's forehead. Her body slumped forward and her hands released the reins of her horse before she slid out of the saddle and dropped to the ground amidst the dancing hooves of the horses. Dan, dazed and breathless from the blow that had knocked him down, rose to his knees and dived for his gun belt. But Keaton wheeled his horse, and Dan looked up at the menacing barrel of the pistol again as his hand groped just inches short of his own gun.

Then a rifle cracked from near the ponderosa, and Keaton's horse reared and struck at air. The sheriff's eyes leaped wildly as they sought the possessor of the rifle that had whistled the bullet past his head. The rifle cracked again, and Keaton grunted but barely flinched as crimson oozed through the waist of his torn shirt. But the assailant had bought Dan his break. His fingers closed on the service revolver now. With the sheriff's attention diverted just long enough, Dan took unhurried aim and squeezed the trigger. The bullet that smashed through the sheriff's jaw and exited at the base of his skull lifted him out of his saddle and dropped him stone dead on the ground.

The horses had raced away by the time Dan stood up, his pistol dangling loosely in his hand. He looked back over his shoulder to see Megan step out from behind the pinto with the rifle, his Winchester, cradled in her arms. She walked slowly toward him as he stared at her in disbelief.

Then he heard Liz moan behind him, and he turned away to where she lay supine on the ground not far from where the sheriff stared skyward with blank, sightless eyes that seemed frozen in his blood-smeared twisted face.

He hesitated and turned back to Megan. "Meg, are—"

"I'm fine," she said. "You'd better see to Liz."

He knelt down and placed a hand on Liz's cheek, caressing it gently as he might a piece of delicate china. She was alive, her bosom rising and falling steadily as she slept there. Her eyes fluttered and then opened, and she looked up at him, her eyes uncomprehending.

"Dan?"

"Yes."

"Keaton? Where?"

"Dead."

"I'm glad. I didn't want him to kill you, Dan. Please believe that much."

"I do. You stopped him from it."

Dan bolted upright, and his grip tightened instinctively on the pistol as a horse's hooves thudded again in the yard. It was Clay Sutherly, who appeared to rein in and dismount in a single motion before he rushed to Liz Dunkirk's side, panic written on his ashen face. "Liz, is she—"

"She'll be all right," Dan said. "She took a blow on her head from Keaton's gun barrel."

Sutherly glanced over at Sheriff Keaton's prone form where droning flies were beginning to feast now. "It looks like somebody ended it before I did," he said matter-of-factly.

"Clay," Liz said, her voice drifting, "what are you doing here?"

"I came here to find you. I didn't know where you were, but I thought you might be here like you were the other times. I didn't expect to ride into this."

"Leave me alone, Clay."

Sutherly placed a hand behind her back and helped Liz into a sitting position. "Just sit here a minute," he said. "I want to talk to Mr. McClure a spell, and then we'll head home."

Sutherly stood up and motioned Dan to join him some distance away from Liz. "What is it?" Dan asked.

"There won't be any more raids," Sutherly said, nodding toward Keaton. "The man who was responsible is dead."

"But Keaton and Liz were partners of sorts," Dan said.

"Can you prove that?"

"They admitted it to me. My testimony to that would be some proof."

"That wouldn't be enough."

"It might be," Dan said.

"What would it accomplish? It won't bring back the dead."

"No, but it would carry out justice, and if she's not brought to trial, what's to say she won't do something like this again?"

"I'm to say," Sutherly said.

"You sound quite positive."

"Mr. Dunkirk's dead. We found him this morning; he died in his sleep. That's why I was looking for Liz . . . to tell her about her father."

"I see."

"I'm sole trustee of the Dunkirk enterprises now. It's up to me whether Liz ever owns the Diamond D or any part of it in her own right."

"That's a lot of power."

"You're damned right it is. And I'll use it, but within the boundaries of the law."

Dan still did not like Sutherly, but he found himself respecting the man. If anybody could handle Liz Dunkirk—and that was doubtful—Sutherly could.

"I'll have to think on it," Dan said noncommittally. But he knew now that the bloodshed was over, he would not turn against Liz Dunkirk. She had claimed a part of him that would not let him do it.

Only after Clay Sutherly had turned away and moved to Liz's side, had Dan searched out Megan who stood quietly near the building site, gazing, so it seemed, at the stakes and strings that outlined the foundation. He walked over to his gun belt, holstered his revolver, left it lying in the dust, and walked up the gentle slope to join Megan.

"Meg?" he said as he came up behind her.

She turned and faced him, and he could see that her eyes were drinking in his image. He took her into his arms and pulled her supple body close, stroking her silky black hair as she pressed her face against his chest.

"When did it happen?" he asked.

"It started on the way over. At first everything was a blur, but it kept getting better. I didn't say anything because I wasn't sure. Things are still a little fuzzy."

"You saw well enough to put a bullet in Keaton."

"But it took two shots," she said apologetically, "and I was aiming for his chest. I can shoot better than that."

He kissed the top of her head. "I'm sure you can."

"Dan, Liz Dunkirk . . . what's going to become of her?"

"I don't know."

"I know you cared for her, though," Megan said.

"Once. But does it matter?"

She was silent for a moment. "No, it doesn't matter . . . not now." She pulled away and looked up at him with clear, moist eyes and smiled hesitantly. "Do you want to show me where our room is?" she asked motioning toward the home site.

"I'd be delighted. Come with me, and I'll give you the grand tour of our new home."

He took Megan's hand in his and led her along the perimeter of the stakes. Then they stopped and looked over the stretched string. "This is the front entrance," he announced. "Double doors, wide enough for us to enter together."

About the Author

Ron Schwab is the author of the popular Western series, *The Blood Hounds, The Law Wranglers*, *The Coyote Saga*, and *The Lockes*. His novels *Grit* and *Old Dogs* were both awarded the Western Fictioneers Peacemaker Award for Best Western Novel, and *Cut Nose* was a finalist for the Western Writers of America Best Western Historical Novel.

Ron and his wife, Bev, divide their time between their home in Fairbury, Nebraska and their cabin in the Kansas Flint Hills.

For more information about Ron Schwab and his books, you may visit the author's website at www.RonSchwabBooks.com.

www.ingramcontent.com/pod-product-compliance
Lightning Source LLC
Chambersburg PA
CBHW061130200626
46817CB00016B/587